THE WIDOWER'S GIRLFRIEND

FAKING IT SERIES - SWEET ROMANCE

MARIKA RAY

THE WIDOWER'S GIRLFRIEND

Copyright 2019 Marika Ray

ISBN-13:
978-1-950141-00-5 (Ebook Edition)
(Print Edition)

Major thanks to these fabulous ladies:
Proofreader: **Judy's Proofreading**
Cover Artist: **Amanda Walker**

INTRODUCTION

Sometimes you have to fake it till you make it, in life and in matters of the heart.

Walker

I practically have *Widower* stamped on my forehead as a speaker traveling the world talking about my experience losing my wife to cancer as newlyweds. Which has always suited me just fine. Until a woman all wrong for me jumpstarts my heart with her comical bad luck at the airport. If I help her out, even for just this weekend, will I also have to throw away my lucrative career as the permanently grieving husband?

Jemma

This final yearly trip with my old friends from high school has gone from bad to worse with a broken suitcase handle and my clothes strewn all over the baggage belt. Tall, dark, and handsome has witnessed all my humiliation with that condescending smirk, yet somehow I crave more time with this total stranger. When he offers to get my so-called friends off my back, who am I to say no?

But somehow between fake kisses and real conversation, the lines blur on what's pretend and what's true love. But what happens in Colorado, has to stay in Colorado. Doesn't it?

The Faking It series books are all stand alone sweet romances about fake relationships turning out to be more real than ever suspected. When true love is on the line, you can't fake your feelings...

1

alker

My phone pings from my carry-on briefcase, its incessant chirping driving me crazy already. I had a cup of coffee at home while I pulled on my wool suit, but clearly, I need another. Early mornings don't normally annoy me like this, but lately, I've been feeling like my life is out of control once again. Case in point: I'm at LAX, one of the busiest airports in the United States at 6 a.m. on a Monday headed to speak at a conference in Denver, Colorado, in February. Clearly, I didn't book this flight or I would have valued my love of sleep and sunshine more than yet another speaking gig. I need to have a word with my assistant.

I check the Rolex on my wrist that my father gave me and see I have enough time to pop into the line at the coffee cart before my flight starts boarding. That is, if the lady in front of me at the entrance to the security line gets her act together.

"Oh crap," she mutters under her breath while struggling to flip her suitcase over. I feel the tugging of a smile, even though her mishap means my window for coffee gets smaller and smaller.

The wheels on her rolling suitcase don't seem to be functioning so instead of trying to fix it, she resorts to dragging the ugly bag while we snake through the line leading to the security checkpoint. Her huge purse starts to slide off her shoulder and she pauses to shove it back up before yet again dragging her suitcase.

When she makes the turn at the first bend in the queue, I get a glimpse of her face.

And what a face it is.

She's gorgeous, with cornflower blue eyes, flushed cheeks, and blonde hair that keeps slipping onto her face and getting stuck in the lip gloss that highlights her pouty lips. My smile grows and my gaze locks onto her like we're the only two people in the huge airport.

I'm startled by her beauty and then I'm startled that I gave her beauty more than tepid appreciation. My wife died eight years ago, and though I'll always miss her like a part of me is missing, I'm not still in the throes of the grief process either. I've worked hard to move my way through the grieving phases in a healthy manner. Though I've dated a bit the last few years, and even with all the local women in Newport Beach, CA, who fit society's definition of beauty, I haven't been genuinely interested in anyone yet. I was beginning to think my grief broke something inside of me.

"Oh!" The extended handle on her suitcase pulls out of its slot altogether, the case falling over onto the floor with a loud bang. She scrambles to pick it back up, her face ablaze. She barely gets a hand on it when her purse slides off her shoulder again, swinging her off-balance with the weight of all the junk women put in their purses. By the time she's teetering and about to go down, I get to her side. I grab an elbow pin-wheeling wildly and pull her back to center, the force of my tug sending her into my chest.

"Wha—" She looks at my chest in bewilderment, before her gaze rises to my face. Her eyes finally lock on mine and the airport recedes completely, leaving the two of us in our own little universe.

A beat or two goes by, both of us speechless, for probably very different reasons. My brain freezes, and for once, I'm out of words.

The startled look fades out of her face, replaced by a polite smile that looks practiced. I much prefer the honesty of her flusterment. That thought alone pulls me out my fog and brings me back to the busy day that awaits me. If I'd only let go of the strange woman I still have in my grasp.

"You may want to consider a new suitcase." I smirk down at her sorry excuse for luggage and pry my fingers off her arm. A step back and the noise of travelers rushing around us hits my conscience.

If it's even possible, she blushes harder and retrieves her bag, still awkwardly holding the broken handle, evidence of the shoddy condition of her luggage. Once she has everything, she looks back up at me, fake smile firmly in place.

"Ah, but then what would build my character, you know?" She winks and walks past me, her bag dragging along the floor, a startling counterpoint to her confident gait. Head held high, she keeps winding through the line.

After picking my jaw up off the floor, I follow quickly behind her. I'm not sure what affects me more: the lighthearted wink or the witty retort I wasn't expecting. Either way you bet I'm going to enjoy watching her go through security. A few people snuck into the line between us, so thankfully I don't look like a creep following her.

I've completely forgotten about my beloved cup of coffee as I see her bumble her way through the checkpoint. She nearly falls over again trying to get her boots off to walk through the metal detector. Heads turn and a bubble of irritation grows in my gut as I see it's mostly men looking at her. With appreciation.

I roll my eyes, realizing I just did the same thing, but that was different.

Besides, she's too young for me. She's barely a full-fledged adult based on her looks and her choice of ridiculous luggage. I may only be thirty-four, but I feel ancient, having gone through the wringer when my late wife got sick. I need to stop looking and I definitely need to stop touching her.

Decision made, I look away and focus on getting myself through security and then hunting down the coffee line. With two minutes to spare, I get my black coffee and race to my gate. They're just calling all first-class passengers to board when I walk up and slide right into the short line.

"Welcome aboard, Mr. James." The female attendant scans the barcode on my phone and gives me the extra wide smile they reserve for first-class passengers. When I started making decent money a few years ago, I decided to indulge in more leg room and better food every time I flew. Which was often, based on my speaking schedule. At six foot four, the extra leg room was almost a necessity. I didn't feel guilty about the added expense, but I made sure to retain an appreciation for everything that came with the upgrade.

Settled into my plush chair, I stow my laptop bag below the seat in front of me and rest my head back, eyes closed. There's plenty of time on the flight to go through my presentation and make sure I'm ready to go. I've given this presentation dozens of times before, but since I'm being paid to make it, I always take the time to make sure I give it perfectly. Just a few short years ago, I was the grieving man, searching for any help that could get me through that dark time. To give anything less than my best would be a disservice to people who really need me.

I take a few deep breaths, visualizing the view of the beach from my front deck, feeling the ocean breeze on my skin and the sound of the seagulls swooping down for their early morning breakfast. Today's flight didn't leave room for my normal morning meditation, but that's the thing about meditation: you can do it anywhere.

That is, unless you're on a full airplane and a loud, persistent scratching noise pierces the air. I open one eye and see the lady from security entering the plane, bag dragging loudly behind her. A flight attendant intercepts her.

"I'm sorry, miss. We're out of bulkhead space. I have to ask you to check your bag. I can take it for you right here."

I see her chest rise and fall on a big sigh. I have to hand it to her, she handles the bad news well. She simply hands her bag over with a nod and continues down the aisle.

She looks around to find her aisle number, her gaze snagging on mine before darting away. The way she bites her bottom lip makes me feel smug, knowing she recognizes me.

I close my eyes again and swear I feel her as she passes me, her light perfume tickling my nose and washing away all hopes of meditating. Then she's gone and I go through all the reasons I need to stop thinking about her, foremost being I'm a locally recognized widower who's made a nice living off of my blog, which turned into a monetized YouTube channel, then a book deal, TV appearances, and then a speaking tour across the country.

Men who make a living as widowers can't be seen chasing after women.

Career suicide.

Plus, I'm not interested in a young woman, pretty as she may be, who hasn't been tested by life like I had. Depth of character and maturity were high on my list of character traits in an acceptable woman. This lady? She couldn't possibly yet possess them.

A loud thunk, followed by a commotion, breaks into my thoughts. I spin around and poke my head out into the aisle, seeing the same woman grappling with her oversized handbag, the one that's currently on the ground and not in the overhead like it's supposed to be. Several bystanders have offered their help, wanting to get the deadly weapon into the overhead bin before she bumbles it again.

The woman is a walking disaster. A bark of laughter escapes before I can muffle it, the sound echoing down the aisle. Her head swivels and she sees me staring at her, a wide grin on my face. She ducks her head and sits down, swallowed by rows of packed seating behind me.

I settle back into my seat and chuckle. I may not have welcomed this early flight, but the joy of watching her navigate an airport like a grown-up was well worth the early alarm. Once we're airborne, I abandon all thoughts of meditating and get out my laptop instead. I need to ground myself in my message and remember why I'm here on this plane: to help people get through the grieving process.

Definitely not to flirt with gorgeous young women.

emma

It's like I have butter for hands. Or perhaps just the worst luck in all of southern California. I don't even want to be here, or spend the money to travel to Colorado, or be inadvertently entertaining the entire plane as I make a fool of myself. This is why I work with kids. They bumble things all the time. My behavior is normal to them.

Clearly it's not normal to the tall gorgeous man who's been front and center to all my mishaps this morning. The one that just laughed at me from his cushy seat in first class.

And that, ladies and gentlemen, is why I'm still single.

At least, according to my mother and my big brother. They've tried to help me with my klutzy ways over the years, to no avail, as I'm sure everyone could see. My mother laments my two left feet, going so far as to sign me up for ballet in my younger years to work on my gracefulness. I was the only kid in history to get kicked out of that ballet company. Even though I said I was sorry a million times, the teacher didn't find a broken nose a forgivable offense. My mom couldn't have afforded the classes for very long anyway, so as far as I could see it, I was simply saving her hard-earned money.

But there is a part of me that really wants a companion. Someone who will overlook my daily foibles and love me for who I am. Where my mother and brother are always trying to change me, my forever love would embrace my clumsiness as an irreplaceable character quirk. That, and he'd work just as hard as me to build a life for us and our children.

Which is why I shouldn't be sitting here fanning myself over Mr. High and Mighty in first class. I'm sure he wouldn't recognize hard work if it smacked him in the face.

"Might consider a new bag..." I mutter under my breath. *Thanks, genius. It never occurred to me that I owned a suitcase that had seen better days.* Unfortunately, some of us have to pull extra shifts just to pay for inflated housing costs in southern California and we don't have money left over for nice things like bags that actually have working wheels or handles that stay attached to the darn bag.

"Miss?"

I pull myself out of my musings and see a flight attendant waiting for an answer to a question I didn't even hear. "I'm sorry. What did you say?"

Her smile freezes, locked onto her face like her job depends on it. "What would you like to drink?"

"Oh! Um, coffee, please."

She shuffles down the aisle collecting orders while I pull out my latest romance novel. I don't have many indulgences, having just become a physician's assistant a little over a year ago. I have student loans to pay alongside those housing costs. No running home to live with Mom going on here; I'm determined to make it on my own. But romance novels are a must and I save up my pennies for the really good ones in paperback.

Lifting the book to my nose, I take a good whiff. There's nothing like the scent of paper and ink to warm me up inside on a chilly day. And nothing says vacation like a new paperback, am I right?

The man next to me shifts away and gives me a weird look. Guess he doesn't appreciate a good happy ever after like I do. Ignoring him, I dive into my romance, transported to a Hawaiian island with a sassy heroine and an impossibly rich and handsome man the more words I read. An elbow jab pulls me back to the airplane hurtling through the skies. The flight attendant is holding a cup of coffee, waiting for me to take it from her.

The steam is drifting out of the cup and luring me in. "Thank you," I tell her sweetly. Coffee and a good book. Now there's true paradise.

I took up pleasure reading to take my mind off stressful things going on in my life, starting in college. At any time, I can open a book and get lost in a different world. A good book is particularly helpful when a patient of mine dies. Considering I work in a pediatric cancer hospital, that happens more often than I ever like to think about. Each little person I work with takes up a section of my heart, ripping it in two should they not overcome the disease. Nothing can make a child's death easier, so I escape.

The heroine's sass reaches a level even the muscled hero can't take and they've momentarily broken up by the time I hear the captain's voice come on overhead, telling us to stow our belongings and fasten our seatbelt. Slapping the book closed, I take one last gulp of coffee, getting a mouthful of cold liquid and coffee grounds. I grimace, looking to my left at the sleeping guy blocking my exit out of the row. The flight attendant is checking we all have our seatbelt on. Nothing to do but swallow it, hoping the extra caffeine gives me the jolt I need to face my old friends when we land.

Everyone stands in a rush when the ding sounds, nearly trampling each other to get our bags out of the overhead bins. Then we wait. And wait some more. By the time I make it off the plane, my nerves are frazzled and I wonder for the hundredth time why I agreed to go on this trip with friends from high school who I haven't even remained close with. I get two weeks' vacation a year. Why did I agree to spend a week of it with them?

"Excuse me, which baggage claim area is States Airlines?" I went to the bathroom and then came out not seeing anyone from my flight. I'm also severely turned around in this unfamiliar airport. The bored attendant points down to the right so I nod my thanks and make my way to the round belts in that area.

I spot the handsome man from earlier standing by a belt with his phone out, reading from the screen like he's Mr. Important. The red light above the carousel starts flashing and a warning buzz lets us all know it's about to start spewing out bags.

The first bag down the shoot and onto the belt is mine.

How do I know?

My lacy bra, the one that I bought on a whim a few months back when I was excited about a blind date—don't ask—and never saw the light of day, is spilling out the side of the suitcase. I run up, push a man out of the way, panic stealing my manners and freezing my brain. All I can think is that I have to get my bag off the belt ASAP before it goes all the way around showing off my bra to every passenger on the plane.

I grab the handle, the only one still connected to the bag, and pull it off the belt with all the muscle I've built lifting patients and moving beds. The suitcase flies off the belt, but spills open at my feet. The zipper is hanging off the bottom, having been ripped off at some point in transportation.

"Seriously?" Hands on hips, I address my bag, like it might just offer up an apology for being a lousy excuse for a suitcase. My face feels like it's on fire and to make matters worse, I feel a single drop of sweat slip down my back. I'm totally flustered and I haven't even met up with my friends yet.

I plop my purse on the ground and crouch down to stuff my clothes and toiletries back into the suitcase in a jumbled mess, completely unconcerned with wrinkles at this point. A shadow covers me and for a split second I actually think the end is near for me. I've been brought down to this level by a silly suitcase and now the Reaper is here for me.

Did I mention I work around kids all day?

"Need some duct tape?" The Reaper speaks and his velvety voice sounds a whole lot more delicious than I would have guessed. I raise my gaze only to find the handsome stranger standing above me, a roll of gray duct tape extended in my direction. A waft of woodsy cologne floats across and I inhale like a starving woman.

Figures he'd be the one to come to my rescue.

I nod gratefully and take the tape. "Thank you. That should help." Now that my clothes are all safely inside where they should be, I wrap the tape around the suitcase and get it closed tighter than the decades-old zipper. I ignore all the stares I can feel on my back as everyone feels sorry for the girl with the exploding luggage.

When I stand back up, he's still there, eyeing my suitcase dubiously, which I totally get. It's been nothing short of a disaster today. But it's not like he has to help me. It's my problem, not his.

"Thank you for the tape." I hand it back and smile widely, hoping he takes the apology for what it really is: goodbye.

His gaze moves over my face, his eyes crinkling and the smirk making a reappearance. "You got a little something…" He gestures toward his mouth and my eyes widen.

I swipe across my mouth, but he just shakes his head, the smirk getting smirkier and my embarrassment ratcheting up several notches. "What is it?"

"Did you have coffee this morning?" he asks.

I run my tongue over my teeth and immediately feel grunge between my two front teeth. I roll my eyes and try to explain, the whole time keeping my teeth from showing while I speak. "I did, but the last sip was straight States Airlines coffee grounds. It's in my teeth, isn't it?"

The smirk finally leaves and I get a blinding smile. "It really is."

My stomach is doing somersaults. I hook a finger over my shoulder then remember to continue covering my mouth. "Okay, well, thanks for the heads-up and I'll just go die a silent death over at the taxi line. Thanks again for the tape." I can't even look him in the eye, my mortification is so complete.

With coffee grounds in my teeth and duct tape holding my suitcase together, I throw my shoulders back and walk out of the Denver airport like I really do have my life together.

Who needs a tall, dark, and handsome man anyway?

3

alker

She's killing me.

Not only is she gorgeous, but she's a highly entertaining walking disaster. When I handed her the duct tape I grabbed from the Information desk and saw the food in her teeth, I was charmed. Then she used wit to talk her way through the embarrassment and I was intrigued. Now, as I watch her walk out of the airport like a princess leaving her kingdom, I can't help but remember the lacy pink bra that escaped her suitcase. Of course, those thoughts naturally lead to thoughts of what she'd look like *in* the undergarment and I scramble to think of something else. Anything else to wipe that from my brain.

It's understandable. I haven't been married for eight years. Which feels like a lifetime. I've almost forgotten what it feels like to be attracted to a warm-blooded female. I didn't make a conscious decision to remain celibate after my wife died, but it happened anyway. After loving someone and losing them to a disease that never should have happened to one so young, I couldn't even fathom entering into a relationship with someone on a surface level. I gave up all ability to handle surface-level conversations when I had to plan my wife's funeral at the age of twenty-six.

But something about this blonde woman with the failed attempts at adulting in the airport is grabbing my attention. She's making me want a relationship again. Which is both a relief and terrifying. Talking about moving on and actually moving on are two totally different animals. Especially when I have my sights set on a woman who clearly hasn't been tested by the world on any kind of deep level. We'd never work out, I just know it.

I grab my bag off the conveyer belt—all in one piece I might add—and walk out to the line of taxis waiting to pick up passengers. The blonde is a few people ahead of me in line and I use the time to observe her and try to come up with the reasons she intrigues me on a deeper level.

She's currently talking with a mom and her young daughter ahead of her in line. The little girl is sucking her thumb, but the second the blonde starts talking to her she drops the thumb and smiles up at her like they're instant best friends. The sight tugs at heartstrings I didn't know existed. I never got a chance to have children with my wife and if I don't speed things up in the dating department, I'll never have the chance.

Strangely, it never bothered me before.

"The Hilton off 14th Street, please." It's her turn and she's about to lift her suitcase into the cab's trunk. The driver rushes around to help her and I see his eyes widen comically when he sees the duct tape. "Don't ask..." she tells him with a quick headshake.

I bite back a groan and move forward, oblivious to everyone else in line ahead of me. "I'm going to the same hotel. Mind if we share?"

Her head whips up and she freezes for a moment. Her mouth tips up in a wry smile. "Sure you want to take that chance?"

I frown. "What do you mean?"

She tilts her head. "Well, I don't know. The way my luck is going, this cab will get a flat tire or something on the way to the hotel."

I can't help but grin, my body working on instinct here. The minute I asked to join her cab, I wasn't engaging my brain any longer. "I'm willing to take that chance."

She shrugs. "You've been warned!" She drops into the cab and scoots over, the open door being all the invitation I need.

The driver is looking at me expectantly so I place my bag in the trunk and hurry to get in. As soon as the door slams shut I want to jump back out. What am I doing prolonging my time with her? I have ten different reasons for not pursuing anything further and not one reason to be here, right next to her, where I can smell her flowery perfume and see how she cracks her knuckles when she's nervous.

And yet, here I am.

"I'm Jemma Reed, by the way." She glances at me and then stares at the road ahead. "Figured since you've fixed my bag, spotted food in my teeth, and have basically seen me at my worst, you might as well know my name."

I smile at the side of her face. Jemma. A perfect name for her. She *is* quite rare, just like a gem. Her eyes slide over to look at me, gauging my reaction to her introduction. Maybe wondering if I'm an ax murderer sent to complete her crappy day.

"Nice to meet you, Jemma. I'm Walker." I extend my arm and she slowly slides her hand into mine. An intimate jolt of awareness runs through me, so I give her hand a quick squeeze and let go. The seat cushion groans as I lean back into my corner of the tattered back seat. "Are you in Colorado for fun or business?" It's the kind of mundane question two strangers would ask that'll get us back on the right track.

She unzips her puffy vest, taking it off and setting it on top of her purse by her feet. The cab driver is blasting the heat, which is nice, but totally unnecessary right now. We both seem to be a bit overheated. I follow suit and take off my fleece-lined leather jacket.

"For fun. Hopefully." She rolls her eyes and smiles, loosening the scarf around her neck. "You?"

I seem to be mesmerized by her disrobing, wondering what's next to come off. When she settles back in her seat and folds her arms across her chest, I bring my gaze back to her face and see her looking at me with those big eyes. "Um, business. Definitely." I let a beat pass, not wanting to get into why I'm here because that always leads to a long explanation about my late wife. Not really a topic I want to get into right now. "If you're here for fun, you must love skiing, huh?"

She laughs, her face dancing with joy. Her broad smile is on full display and I like the way she doesn't cover it up. "Nope! I can't stand skiing actually, or snow for that matter. The location was not my choice, so I'm going to make the most of it while staying indoors. By a large fire, preferably."

I find myself grinning, agreeing with her assessment of snow. "I hear you on that. I'm all about beaches and sunny skies, personally."

Before she can reply, her phone starts singing the Micky Mouse Clubhouse theme song. I'm instantly curious why a grown woman chose that as her ringtone, but then again, she does look pretty young. Maybe she never grew out of her Disney phase.

Jemma digs through her purse, pulling out a cell phone charger, her brown leather wallet, and a variety of pens with pharmaceutical names on the sides, placing them on the seat bench between us. Finally finding her phone, she mouths "sorry" before tapping the answer button.

"Hi, Diana!" she answers with a smile, but then starts running her thumb nail up and down the outside seam of her jeans, a nervous habit I doubt she's aware of. She listens, nodding her head occasionally. I can hear a woman's voice chirping on the other end of the line, talking a million miles a minute, not letting Jemma get a single word in for several minutes.

"Yep, I know. I'm in a cab right now." She bites her lip and listens again before answering. "Yeah, sorry, but—" She nods. "Okay, bye."

Hanging up her phone, she slides it into her purse and looks out the windshield, a frown marring her beautiful features.

4

emma

"God, Jay, why did you book such a late flight? We're all here, ready to go out, and now we have to wait on you. Are you at least close?"

Diana's high-pitched voice in my ear is like nails on a chalkboard. What happened to polite conversation like "hey, how was your flight? Glad you got here safely?" I guess I should have expected this kind of reception.

"Yep, I know, I'm in a cab right now." I glance out the window, not knowing where I am, but thinking I'm only ten minutes or so from the hotel.

"I'll see if I can get the girls to wait, but I don't know. It's kind of putting a damper on our plans..." She trails off, like waiting ten more minutes is a big deal when we're supposed to be here all weekend together.

"I know, I'm sorry, but—"

"Oh—gotta go. Call you back in a second!"

The loud click, followed by silence, cuts off my goodbye. I pull the phone from my ear and grit my teeth. Honestly, they're so rude. I keep thinking things will get better or they'll magically change back into the girls I went to high school with: sweet, funny, and considerate. But year after year of these girls' trips and it's not getting better. It's only getting worse.

"That went well," Walker adds dryly.

Crud, I forgot for a minute he was in the cab with me. I plaster on a smile—I'm good at faking it—and turn to him. "Yeah, my friends are kind of hyper. They just want to go, go, go!"

He doesn't smile back, just studies me as I keep that smile in place. What is he even doing here with me? I nearly swallowed my tongue when he hopped up and wanted to share the taxi with me. I'd made a total fool of myself all morning in front of him, and yet here he was, purposely signing up to spend more time with a total klutz. It didn't make sense, which made me more nervous than I should be. That and he was crazy handsome.

"Hmm. I have some energetic friends like that, but they're still kind."

My eyes widen and my cheek muscles fail me as the smile slides off my face. How could he have guessed that? "Did you hear my conversation?"

He frowns, the two lines between his eyes deepening. "No, but I heard your end of it."

That makes me feel slightly better, but still exposed. I'm not proud of how my friends treat me, and I'm certainly not happy about it, but hearing him judge my friendships when he and I are perfect strangers doesn't sit well with me. "They're not that bad, really. You'd have to know them."

His frown lines smooth out and his lips hint at a smile. "Yeah, I guess you're right."

Satisfied he dropped it, I nod and swivel to look outside. I mean, he's not telling me anything I don't already tell myself. But I've known these three girls since high school. At what point do you give up and sever a ten-plus-year friendship? There's history there, and inside jokes, and a shared background that just wasn't repeatable now that I'm an adult. Besides, everyone deserves a second chance. Sometimes a third or fourth. Right?

I spin around again, my indignation making my mouth speak when I should have just stayed quiet and left well enough alone. "You know, they were there for me in high school. I wasn't one of the rich kids with the name brands and a fancy car when I turned sixteen. Those girls took me under their wing and made me one of their own, which is pretty much what every insecure teenager wants in high school. So yeah, they might be a little bratty now that we're adults, but I owe them, okay?"

My tirade ends and silence fills the cab, even the driver not wanting to draw any attention to himself in this argument. Walker is staring me down, his brown eyes darting across my face, absorbing my words. His face is serious, but he seems to be really listening to me, a quality that's rare among the people I hang out with. I still regret explaining myself to him. He's a virtual stranger, so why am I dumping all my personal drama on him?

"Sounds like they played a key part during that time of your life." Walker nods yet somehow I know he's not done. "I'm a firm believer that we should always be choosing who to surround ourselves with. And I also believe that someone right for you ten years ago isn't necessarily right for you today. Some relationships grow together over the years and some break apart. Trying to cling to a friendship that isn't right for you now does you a grave disservice."

Now it's my turn to absorb his words, thinking he has a good point. I slump a bit in the seat, the fight leaving me. "I hear what you're saying, and it's not far off from what I've been saying in my own head. But it's easier said than done. How do you cut off a long-term friendship like that? At what point is enough enough?"

Walker tilts his head. "Only you can decide that. But if I may, I would suggest you check in with how you feel when you're around them. True friends should lift you up, not make you feel badly about yourself."

I have to admit, it's not bad advice. Giving him a cheeky grin, I ask, "What are you? A psychologist or something?"

He barks out a laugh. "No, not a psychologist. Just someone who's had to do a lot of soul searching."

Before I can ask him what he means by that, my phone rings again. The ringtone makes me think of my precious little patients, but the caller ID makes me cringe. Diana's calling back.

"Hi, Diana." I bring the phone to my ear and hope Walker can't hear her voice. She's nearly shouting now, talking over wind noise in the background.

"Jay, we couldn't wait. We're taking an Uber to a little spa a few blocks over. The boys booked us three massages. Isn't that super sweet? Oh my gosh, workaholic, get a husband already so you can join in on the fun. We'll see you after our massage, okay?"

"Um, okay, I'll see you in a bit."

"Gotta go, bye!"

I put my phone back in my bag and roll my eyes. "Okay, they've definitely gotten worse over the years."

Walker chuckles and the rumble of his laugh rolls through me like a tangible thing, warming up everywhere the conversation with my friends left me cold.

"Get a husband already?" Walker leans closer, his eyes dancing by repeating my friend's ridiculous comment.

I feel the blush steal across my cheeks. "Oh, you heard that, did you?"

"I think the car next to us heard that, yeah."

Rubbing my hand over my face, I sneak a peek at him. "So...I guess that conversation makes my decision a little clearer."

He lifts his eyebrows. "Hard to believe they used to be kind and considerate. Maybe their husbands are a bad influence?"

I shake my head. "No, they're actually pretty cool guys. I think college just sent us all on different paths. I was studying hard while they were partying hard. And then by the time I graduated, work took over and I rarely saw them. That's why we made up the annual girls' trip: to be certain we all make time for each other, even when life gets busy."

The driver honks his horn and mutters under his breath. Looking outside, it seems we're stuck in a bit of a traffic jam. Secretly, I'm pleased to get some extra time to talk to this captivating stranger-not-stranger.

Walker has an expression on his face I can't place. "So, no husband in the works to appease your friends?"

I huff out a laugh. "No, definitely not. No time to find one, I guess. Sure would make my life easier though if I did. Heck, even a prospect would get them off my back." I shrug my shoulders. "Oh well, not the end of the world. Especially if I'm considering distancing myself from them in the future."

We lapse into easy silence, each of us looking out the passenger windows, assessing how far away we are from the hotel and if we might actually get there with all this traffic. Funny how my friends have already rubbed off on me, their judgement making me change how I naturally feel. I don't mind being single. I enjoy my career immensely and I refuse to settle for just any guy, but admitting my single status to Walker gave me a twinge of embarrassment. Like I should apologize for not following society's expectations and landing a husband already at the ripe old age of twenty-eight.

"Wanna get a little crazy this weekend?" I swing my startled gaze over to Walker, taking in his pressed trousers and button-down dress shirt. If I'm not mistaken, a Rolex peeks out from under his starched cuff. Dark brown oxfords complete his businessman look, one that's stylish, but not on par with a guy looking to "get wild" while out of town. "We could help each other out."

5

alker

Her eyes are guarded, and I haven't even proposed the crazy idea on my mind yet. The minute I heard her friends heckling her about not having a husband, I wanted to step in and help. Why, I don't know. All I know is I seem to have a bit of a 'knight in shining armor' complex like my buddy Jake always tries to tell me. I never believed him until just this minute.

The slump of her shoulders after her friends talked to her physically pained me and I think I can make it better. As a fellow human being, I should offer my assistance, right?

"Now, don't say no immediately, okay?" I lean toward her and if possible, her eyes get even more guarded.

"That makes me want to say no right away, Walker." She lifts an eyebrow and I swear, her hint of sass does more to my gut than her laugh does.

"Just hear me out." I put my hands up to ward off her refusal. "You're thinking this might be your last girls' weekend, and your friends give you grief over being single. I really hate to see people be disrespected—you might even say it's my biggest pet peeve—so I'd like to propose an idea. Why don't we pretend to be a couple and you walk out of your last weekend with these women with your head held high?"

Jemma's frozen and now so am I. I can't believe I just threw that out there, offering my time with a woman I know I shouldn't be around. It's like my body is doing the opposite of what my brain wants. My body's running the show and there's no telling where this thing might end. Like a runaway freight train without breaks.

She shakes her head, eyes closed, nose scrunched. "I'm sorry, what?"

I want her to say yes, more than I've wanted anything in a long time. There's no explaining it to my brain; he's not having it. "I'm here for just this weekend too. I'll come with you to a few things with your girlfriends, we'll pretend to be a couple to get them to quit harassing you, and then we'll part ways when the weekend's over. No harm, no foul."

Her eyes narrow. "Why would you do that?"

I shrug. "I told you. I hate to see someone mistreated. Plus, it might be nice to have a friend while I'm here in Colorado. Gets lonely traveling by yourself all the time."

She chews on her bottom lip again and I clench my fists to keep from pulling it out from under her sharp teeth. "You don't want anything in exchange?"

I shake my head.

"You're not afraid to be around the most uncoordinated woman you've probably ever met?"

Another shake.

"You'll really do it?" Her tone turns hopeful and my body rejoices.

"Yes, I'll really do it."

She squeals and claps, bouncing in her seat. The driver eyes me in the rearview mirror and I know what his expression says. I may be crazy, but I'm a happy crazy now that she's said yes.

I can't help but smile at her excitement. Most women in Newport Beach don't—or can't due to Botox injections—express that much emotion. Casual boredom is the look that's in right now and it's not only refreshing to leave that behind, it's also a nice reminder that the whole world isn't like that. There's hope for a guy like me who just wants a genuine woman to have a deep and meaningful conversation with.

Not that I'm thinking Jemma is that woman, but for the weekend, it might be nice to have a buddy.

"We should probably lay some ground rules." I frown, remembering why I'm here in Denver to start with. I have a presentation on death and grieving to give.

"Oh sure, that's a good idea. That way if you want to bail on this idea, you don't feel pressured into continuing." She nods and pulls her legs underneath her on the bench seat, oblivious to her wet boots getting her jeans dirty.

"No, that's not what I mean. I'm not going to bail on you, but I do have some business obligations while I'm here."

She wrinkles her nose again. "Yeah, why are you here?"

"I'm do—"

"Wait!" She throws her hands up in the air and cuts me off. "Don't tell me if you have to then kill me."

I chuckle. "What? I'm not a spy or here undercover."

She lets her hands fall to her lap. "Just making sure."

Shaking my head at her silliness, I continue. "I'm here to give a speech at a convention. So there will be certain times that I can't be seen with you around the hotel."

She nods sagely. "That's the part you can't tell me or you'll have to kill me."

This girl... "No! It's just the subject matter of my speech means I can't be seen with a woman."

She's back to frowning. Her face is more expressive than anyone I know. "I don't follow. Are you gay?"

Now I'm taken aback. "No, not gay." I guess I should just tell her before she comes up with some bizarre scenario in her imaginative brain. "I'm a widower, giving a presentation on grieving to other widows and widowers."

Her face immediately smooths out and understanding dawns. "I'm sorry to hear that, Walker. How did your wife die?"

This is a question I'm asked all the time. It's something I discuss ad nauseum on my blog and in my book and on my YouTube videos. After awhile, my answer became memorized, devoid of feeling, like each repetition drained a drop more of my grief out of me. But looking into Jemma's eyes and speaking about my late wife is oddly intimate. Like I'm telling the story for the first time.

"Brain cancer. We dated all through college and got married right after graduation. A year later, her frequent migraines were diagnosed: cancer. She had surgery, did all the treatments, ate healthy, did yoga, did everything right. But she still got worse. She held on for almost three years before slipping away in her sleep one night."

Jemma places her hand over mine and squeezes, the gesture made to comfort. I squeeze back and then let go, needing to distance myself from her and her natural magnetism.

Her voice cuts through the quiet. "I can only imagine what that's like. Three years is a long time. She must have fought hard to stay with you."

There's no pity on her face. I would know. I've come to easily identify that expression having seen it on many people's faces over the years. Only understanding, which is more disconcerting when I expect her to not get it.

"Yes, three years was a long time. And yet not long enough."

She gets a soft smile on her face. "I once had a little boy come through my facility. Absolutely determined to beat his lymphoma. You've never seen determination like that. Even when it was clear to everyone he wasn't going to win the fight, he kept telling his parents not to worry. More concerned with his parents' feelings than his own impending death. I don't know what you believe in, but there's no doubt in my mind that little boy is up in heaven still watching over us, telling his parents 'I got this! Don't worry, Mom and Dad!'"

There are tears in her eyes as she tells her story. The feeling is infectious, but I'm also confused. "Where do you work?"

"Hoag's Pediatric Cancer Center in Costa Mesa."

The taxi lurches forward, finding a break in the traffic. I rear back my head. "Wow."

She nods, that same smile making her look younger than someone should be to carry that heavy load of grief. "Yeah, wow is right. I'm a physician's assistant, P.A. for short. I tell people I have hundreds of children."

She winks at her own joke and I shake my head, impressed with her line of work.

And ashamed of myself.

I've badly misjudged her, thinking she was too shallow to hold a conversation with someone like me. This woman's medical knowledge and capacity to both comfort and heal leaves me feeling like a fraud. I'm just a guy blogging about his loss to make himself feel better. She deals with loss of innocent children every day. She should be giving this presentation, not me.

"We're finally here, folks!" the cab driver calls over his shoulder, breaking the moment.

Jemma scrambles to get her vest back on and collect her belongings into her huge purse. Only when she opens the door and the gust of cold air hits me do I spring into action. I hand the driver a couple twenty-dollar bills and hop out to meet her around the car at the trunk.

"Want to write my number down and text me when you know your schedule?"

She fishes her cell phone out of her bag again. "Sure, what is it?"

I recite my number and she calls it. My phone vibrates in my pocket, so I know I have her number now too. Pulling both our bags out of the trunk, I don't know how to say goodbye. Maybe it's better not to say goodbye at all.

I slam the trunk and the cab drives off.

"Hey! I didn't pay him yet!" Jemma waves her arms in the air like that'll get him to see her and come back.

"It's okay, I took care of it." I grab my bag. "Come on. Let's check in before we freeze."

6

emma

My suitcase is heavy, and given the wheels don't work any longer, I have to pick it up and carry it. And Walker is darn tall. His legs eat up the covered driveway and he's in the hotel before I've had a chance to argue about the cab fare. Somehow I think that was part of his plan. Contrary to the state of my bag, I'm not completely destitute. I can pay for my own portion of the cab fare.

"Mr. James! Lovely to see you, sir. Can I get your bag to your room for you?" The bellhop is hovering like a busy bee, acting like the president himself has arrived. Gee, where's my personal bellhop ready to take my exploding bag off my hands?

Walker chuckles, but it sounds different somehow, like he slipped into a different skin the second we left the cab. "No, thank you. I've gotta keep my muscles somehow, huh?"

The bellhop guffaws like Walker's said something particularly hilarious. I mean, I get it. The man's charming and good looking. But he's acting like Walker's some sort of celebrity, which is weird.

"Welcome, Mr. James. We have your room all ready for you. Top floor, beautiful view of the city." The front desk attendant smiles warmly at him from behind her desk and I'm thinking maybe they know each other. I don't like her smile. Something about it rubs me the wrong way.

"Perfect, thank you so much." Walker beams right back at her and there I stand, by myself in the lobby like I'm invisible, wondering what the hubbub is all about.

He pockets his key card and spins around to see me. He's about to say something when two men approach him from the side. He drops my gaze and vigorously shakes their hands while introductions are made and then glances over at me to discreetly make the universal sign to call him, pinkie and thumb extended by his ear. After that, I'm ignored, which is fine by me. I have a room to check into and friends to impress. Yep, totally fine being ignored.

"We'll need to see your ID and a form of payment for incidentals, please." The front desk attendant gives me a practiced smile, one that's several degrees cooler than the one she gave Walker. Practically glacial if I'm being honest.

I hand over my driver's license and my one and only credit card. The snapping of a photo behind me piques my interest. Walker and the two men who greeted him are huddled, one of them with their arm extended, snapping selfies. I frown, not understanding why total strangers would want a selfie together. It's like I've fallen down the rabbit hole and I'm left bewildered in a strange new world like Alice.

"Miss?" The attendant is trying to hand my cards back to me.

"Sorry." I put them back in my wallet and chance a question. "Do you know who that is? Mr. James, I believe they called him?"

Her eyes light up and she leans closer to whisper. "Good looking, right?"

The warmth that flooded my system just minutes earlier in the cab with Walker has dissipated. Like that version of Walker, the one who told me all about his late wife, never existed. "Um, yes, for sure. But why are they taking selfies with him?"

She's frowning at me now, like I've completely lost the plot. "Well, he's pretty famous, you know?"

Mentally, I'm eye rolling at her inability to answer a question without making it a question in return. On second thought, she might make a great therapist.

Then it hits me she's said he's famous. And just like that, all the butterflies and warmth are gone, replaced by a creeping coldness that leaves me wanting nothing to do with Walker. Pretend boyfriend? Not a snowball's chance in hell.

The attendant slides my room key across the counter and I snatch it up. Escape is near. I attempt to get to the bank of elevators, careful to keep my gaze away from Walker. His type loves attention and I'm unwilling to give it to him, even as I have to walk right by him. Of course, my grand exit is marred by my stupid suitcase, the sound of it dragging across the marble floor letting out a screech that brings all eyes to me.

I lift my nose an inch higher in the air and continue on, like I don't feel the weight of their pity stares. Yes, my suitcase is a disaster. Let's move on, shall we?

Jabbing the up button on the elevator panel a little harder than necessary, I remember a particularly sweet little boy two years ago when I first started working full-time at the Cancer Center. He had a rough case of brain cancer and his greatest wish was to meet a professional football player from his local team. After lots of emails back and forth with the player's agent, we had his wish all set up. We knew schedules with celebrities were often tough to stick to, so we didn't tell our patient about his surprise until the day before when we knew for sure it was going to happen.

His excitement was contagious, the entire Center joining him in celebration. The little boy put on his team jersey and waited for hours. Frantic calls and emails behind the scenes on our end went unanswered. The player no-showed. No excuse, no warning. Just left a sick little boy hanging.

Our patient was devastated, crying himself to sleep that night, no amount of consoling from our staff or his family making a dent in his sadness. Later, we found out the football player went and partied too hard the night before, too hung over or strung out the next day to remember where he was supposed to be.

That was the day I decided celebrities did more harm than good. They wielded too much power simply for being able to recite a line on camera or throw a ball downfield. They got paid millions for their skill. Wasn't that enough? Did they need our worship too? For me, the answer was an absolute no.

So finding out Walker was a self-absorbed celebrity? That was a distinct turn-off. A huge red flag telling me to stay away, steer clear, do not pass go. And definitely don't pretend to be his girlfriend for the weekend.

The only problem is the realization that Walker's one of the bad guys makes my heart sink. Takes the wind out of my sails and leaves me deflated. He seemed so genuine when we talked in the taxi. Not self-absorbed at all. Bizarre that my intuition was so off.

The elevator dings its arrival and I hurry to get on, wanting the peace and quiet of my hotel room to sort through my conflicting thoughts. Needing to get myself together before I went to battle with my high school friends.

Just before the doors slide shut, I lift my gaze one last time, the temptation to see Walker again too strong to deny. One last look to remember him by.

He's still talking to the two men, but he's staring straight at me, his intimate gaze so at odds to how I'm feeling about him right now.

And then he winks.

I feel that flutter of his eyelid all the way to the tips of my toes, setting me on fire again.

The doors finally shut and the elevator climbs, the jerk in motion pulling me out of his spell. I'm confused, wondering who the heck this man is, really. The one whose eyes softened as he talked about his late wife, or the one who took a selfie with strangers without a second thought.

One thing I do know: he intrigues me and I'm attracted to him. Plain and simple.

Neither making me happy.

Flashing my key card, I get the door to my hotel room open, stepping inside to a cold room, smelling like an ash tray. Okay, maybe more like a cross between an ash tray and a fish market. A stench that lingers in the nasal passages and permeates clothes.

Just my luck.

I flop down on my bed and stare at the beige ceiling wondering why I'm here. And why am I more nervous about running into Walker again than I am having to go to battle with my friends? I indulge in a ten-minute pity party, spending nine of those minutes going over every word of my conversation with Walker, rather than girding my loins and preparing for my girl-friends to whack me over the head with my single status, how I held them up, and why my purse is from Target and not a designer label.

When I'm more depressed than I can stand, I force myself up, deciding to hang up my clothes and get moving rather than lie here and hate my life. When everything is put away, my phone dings, signally an incoming text.

Diana: Dinner at 7 p.m. at Simon's. Hydrate now!

Oh great. Dinner at a top-rated restaurant won't be cheap. Reminding myself it will be one of the last, since this is the last trip I'll be going on, I pull out a little black dress and eye it on the hanger.

It's cut modestly in the front, but dips quite low in the back.

Plus, the skirt flairs and flutters when I walk, which I find highlights my long legs. It's tasteful (-ish), it's feminine, and I've never had an opportunity to wear it. But when you find the perfect LBD for a great price, you buy it. It's Rule #7 in the women's handbook you're given at birth.

What the handbook doesn't tell you is what to do with handsome men who perplex you and make you feel conflicting things. Which is why I sit in the hotel room chair and spin maniacally, staring out the window to the city streets below. The dizziness is welcome, if only a respite from the confusion that grips my gut.

Text? Or don't text?

My phone lights up when I place my thumb on the wheel, coming to life and taunting me with how easy it would be to text Walker. Then I hear that fake laugh he gave the bellhop and I chicken out, letting the screen go dark. This goes on for several rounds before I get another text from Diana.

Diana: Guess what?? Justine just showed us the bridesmaids' dresses! You're gonna love yours...it's the prettiest shade of pumpkin you've ever seen! Perfect for a fall wedding.

The idea of Justine picking a dress I actually like is preposterous, on par with the chances of them stopping their bashing of my no-husband status. I'm envisioning walking down the aisle in an actual pumpkin costume, which I'd bet next month's salary isn't far from the truth.

It's with thoughts of being the squash-dressed loser at Justine's wedding running through my head that I pick up my phone and find Walker's number.

Before rational thought can re-engage in my brain, I thumb out a message.

Me: Dinner with the girls at 7 p.m. at Simon's. Wanna join me?

I wait a few seconds, but don't see a returning bubble. My foot starts tapping and my palms get sweaty. My phone dings, and I almost drop it, bobbling it clumsily.

Walker: I'll meet you there at 7. ;)

I laugh out loud, more from a need to release this crazed energy than from anything funny. Walker doesn't strike me as the kind of guy to use a winky face, but then again, do I really know him at all?

Biting my lip, I savor the feeling when I formulate what to text back to Diana. It shouldn't give me such a gloating feeling, but there you have it. I'm shallow, I admit. I only wish I could see her face when she reads my text.

Me: Can't wait to see it! PS - Add an extra seat at dinner for my boyfriend.

Bubbles instantly appear after I hit send.

Diana: WHAT?

Diana: Tell me EVERYTHING

Diana: Spill it, woman!

Diana: Hello??

Diana: Oh, that's just cold. You're going to make me wait, aren't you?

Diana: Just tell me this: is he hot? ;)

A winky face from Diana I can understand. But now the similarities between Walker's emoji usage and Diana's makes me wonder what I've gotten myself into. But I really can't dwell on that right now. All I can think about is leaving this friendship on a high note. Like a quarterback retiring after a Super Bowl win.

I feel smug.

And it feels so good.

7

alker

"Hang in there, Clarence. I'll talk tomorrow about what to do with all those guilty feelings." I shake his hand, pat him on the shoulder, and move on to the next group, working the room like the professional speaker I am.

Another attendee snags my attention and tries to tell me their death story. And it's sad. It always is. But at some point, you have to grow a thick skin, otherwise you drown in their sadness, taking it on as your own. I'm not in this for the fame or the fortune, though I will admit that's a nice trickledown effect. I'm in it to help people. To be someone they can talk to at their very lowest point in life. To be the person I didn't have eight years ago.

So I look him in the eye and nod. A frown and a pursed lip when appropriate. A few words of encouragement, a clap on the back. And I let their heartache bounce off me. Heard, but not absorbed.

As I work the room, my thoughts drift to her. Not the "her"

the attendees believe I'm thinking of, the one my whole blog and book is about, but the "her" from today. The one that wormed her way into my brain, intriguing me beyond all explanation.

I'd waffled since we parted ways, hoping I never saw her again to then checking my phone every few minutes to see if she contacted me. And when the text finally came in, I'd wasted no time saying yes, even though my brain was screaming no.

I walk over to a new group, a quick glance at my watch showing I have five minutes before I need to sneak out of this cocktail reception and take an Uber to the restaurant. Guilt immediately eats away at me, for wanting to spend time with Jemma, for wanting to ditch my responsibilities to these grieving people, for planning to speak to a crowd about my late wife while my thoughts all revolve around another woman.

I've never felt like a fraud writing or speaking about the subject of grief. I've always been upfront about not being a professional counselor or psychologist, just a man who was grieving his wife.

Until today.

Until her.

Because it's one thing to talk about moving on, or to think that you have. It's an entirely different thing to actually move on by way of action. A nuance I never understood before. A distinction I needed to explore, for my own sake, and for the sake of the thousands of grieving widows and widowers who looked to me for a roadmap out of the pit of depression.

At exactly ten till seven, I make my apologies and walk out of the ballroom, on the pretense of using the restroom. Instead, I sneak out the side door of the convention center and walk around the outside of the hotel to the lobby. I hand over my ticket to the bellhop and retrieve my jacket while selecting an Uber driver on my phone.

The whole way over to the restaurant, I'm convincing myself this dinner means nothing. I'm just pretending to be her boyfriend to help her out of a rough spot. My heart defies me and continues to race despite my logical explanation of tonight's events.

Before I'm ready, the car pulls up outside Simon's and I see her.

My gaze doesn't waver as I climb out and slam the door behind me. She's beautiful. A black dress clings to her body, the hem high enough to burn the vision into my brain. The heels, the makeup, the softly curled hair. It all adds up to one of the most gorgeous women I've ever seen.

She shifts from foot to foot as I approach. Her shiver is visible from where I stand directly in front of her.

"Let's get you inside." I frown, seeing she's in a jacket, but her bare legs must be freezing in this weather. My hand settles on her elbow and I steer her into the restaurant.

"I thought we should go in together so I stayed outside." Her teeth are chattering and I roll my lips to keep a lecture from coming out. It's winter in Denver. You shouldn't stay outside with bare legs.

"Reservation for Ridgefield?" Jemma asks the hostess.

"Yes, I have you down for five people. Is the rest of your party here?"

"Um, no, not yet. We'll wait here if you don't mind." Jemma smiles, but I can tell it's forced.

We turn around and move to the benches in the waiting area. All I do is lift my eyebrow and she blurts out, "Don't say it! I know they're being rude."

I lift my hands in surrender. "I didn't say anything."

"Mhmm." She gives me a sour look, but then laughs.

I lean my shoulder into her for a moment. "You look beautiful, Jemma."

Her cheeks flush and she looks at me briefly before looking around the restaurant. "Thank you."

"Coat?" I gesture to her jacket, before she spins around and lets me help her out of it. A wide expanse of creamy skin is unveiled as the jacket comes off her back. I start coughing and nearly drop her jacket.

"You okay?" She looks at me over her shoulder, concern in the lines on her face, not realizing she's the cause of my choking.

I pull at my collar and swallow hard. Time to change the subject. I take a seat and nod toward the seat next to me. "Should we get our back story straight before they show up?"

She sits and looks at me puzzled. "What do you mean?"

I shrug. "Well, if we're going to pass our relationship off as believable, we need to know some basic facts about each other, don't you think?"

Her face clears and she nods her head. "Gotcha. Let's see. How about we've been dating for six months and we met at that annual outdoor music concert in Huntington Beach?"

"Sure. What's your favorite color? Pet peeve?" This is somehow more fun than I thought it'd be.

"Turquoise and entitlement. You?"

"Royal blue and judgement with no context."

She wrinkles her nose. "What does that mean?"

"I hate it when people are too quick to judge others when they don't know anything concrete about the other person with which to base their opinion. It's a natural habit for us humans to judge, but the problem is when people judge with no context. Wouldn't you agree?"

She lifts her eyebrows and tilts her head, her long, blonde hair lying on my arm. What I wouldn't give right then to have my jacket off so I could feel that silky curl against my skin. "Who's to say that prior experience doesn't provide enough context for someone to make snap judgements without truly knowing that particular individual? Making quick judgements is a way of protecting one's self, right?"

A smile finds its way onto my face. I wasn't expecting that thought-out response. Which is quite a touché moment considering I'd judged her as being too shallow to have a philosophical discussion. "Valid point. Why entitlement?"

"Everyone wants something for nothing. They want the best paying job without actually having to work hard to get it. They want the privilege without the accompanying responsibility. Life doesn't work that way, or at least, it shouldn't."

Interesting that that's her biggest pet peeve. "What about talent that comes naturally without a lot of hard work? Should that be—"

"Ma'am? Sir? We need to seat you now or we have to release your reservation since it's twenty minutes past." The hostess looks uncomfortable delivering this news. Like she hates to point out that we got dumped by our group. I don't want Jemma feeling bad so I jump up and take control.

"We'd actually love to be seated and order an appetizer."

"Wonderful. Right this way." She spins and walks away.

Pulling Jemma up by the hand, I lace our fingers together and follow the hostess. I can feel Jemma staring at the side of my head, but if we're going to act like boyfriend and girlfriend this weekend, we might as well get started as we mean to go along. Her hand feels soft, my heart enjoying her touch more than I like to admit.

When we reach our table, I let go of her hand reluctantly, pulling back her chair for her. She smiles shyly and sits down, letting me scoot her in. I place her jacket on the back of her chair and take the seat to her left, on the end, so she can sit next to her friends.

Jemma stares at the menu, her cheeks a delightful shade of pink. My arm goes around the back of her chair, my hand dangerously close to touching her exposed back.

From my vantage point, I can see the front of the restaurant, so when I see a group of three women, dressed like a night on the town is in their future, I know the group has arrived.

Placing my hand on Jemma's back, she jumps, but I pull her

toward me anyway. Her eyes widen as I lean in close, our noses just inches away from each other.

"I'm going to kiss you. Okay?" I whisper.

Her eyes widen further, but she gives a quick nod, the permission being all I need to make my move. A move that feels remarkably rusty yet perfectly inevitable. Like she and I were always meant to wind up here, sharing breath, making each other's hearts race in this restaurant in downtown Denver.

The moment my mouth descends to hers, the sound of the diners around us dims, all four non-imperative senses taking a back seat so that all my awareness can focus in on the feel of her lips pressed to mine. The way her body trembles at my touch. The way she gasps, the soft intake of air pulling me in and gripping my chest. The way I feel her move beneath me, actively participating in this kiss to end all kisses.

And just when I think I could stay there forever, feasting on her mouth and breathing her air, someone jostles her and her lips break away. The chair is still under me, but I'm tumbling, adrift without a compass, a game plan, or a coherent thought.

"Jay! How are you?" A tall brunette wraps her arms around Jemma, her perfume nearly choking me.

"Ahhhh!" A high-pitched squeal behind me gets my head swiveling, taking in a short, dark-haired woman with the sparkliest dress I've ever seen. She swoops in and nearly tackles Jemma, pushing the brunette out of the way.

The third, a well put together bleach blonde woman, stands in the aisle, like she can't be bothered to join in on the hug fest and wants everyone in the restaurant to stare at her a bit first anyway.

I recognize her. Well, not *her* exactly, but I recognize her type. The ones with subtle nose jobs, plumped-up lips, and tattooed eyebrows. There're thousands of them living back home near me. And suddenly I understand Jemma's argument about past experience perhaps being enough to help you form a snap judgement that protects you. Because this woman is trouble. I can feel it.

Jemma finally stands and hugs the stiff blonde. Then she introduces me.

"Diana, this is Walker. Walker, this is Diana, Justine, and Amy."

The first two shake my hand limply when I stretch my arm out. Amy, though. She gives me just her fingertips, her eyes appraising me head to toe. And if I'm not mistaken, there's a gleam in her eyes that's decidedly calculating.

They finally sit opposite us and I put my arm back around Jemma's chair, my fingertips playing with the ends of her hair, delighted when I feel her shiver. A devoted boyfriend would be touching her as much as possible and I'm all too happy to play my part to the best of my ability.

Amy's smiling serenely at Jemma, but I can tell she doesn't like that she's been left out of this pertinent information. Gossip hounds can't stand being the last to know all the juicy details. "So, Jemma. How long has this been going on?"

emma

Goodness gracious. What was all that about? We'd been talking about pet peeves and the next thing you know, he's moving in and obliterating all thought with a simple kiss. Okay fine, there was nothing simple about it. My lips are still tingling from it, the taste of him lingering even as I have to dodge questions from my friends. I'm going to have to ask Walker to stop wearing that cologne. It's wrapping me in a bubble of foresty musk mixed with man and stopping all brain function.

"Um, let's see. Six months now, right, honey?" I plaster on what I hope is a believable smile and turn to Walker, begging him with my eyes to help me out.

His hand brushes against my back and his touch zings through my whole body, distracting me and making me forget why I'm even here. His face conforms to a lazy smile the minute I call him "honey," the look making my stomach melt. I like that look. I want more of that look directed my way.

"Yeah, that's about right. The best six months of my life." He winks at me and then turns to my friends.

"I hear you've all been friends since high school. What do you all do now?"

And just like that, Walker's redirected the viper, otherwise known as Amy, to other pastures. It's ingenious really. A move I use a lot with my patients when they have to do a painful procedure. Distract, redirect, or get them talking about themselves.

"I'm a full-time housewife at the moment and there are several charities that I'm involved in," Amy answers smoothly. I raise an eyebrow but remain silent. Amy hasn't volunteered her time since senior year when she had to in order to graduate. More like her husband writes a check every year to some cause, not to do something good, but to get the tax write-off.

"I'm getting married in just a few months!" Justine bursts forth with her news, karate chopping her hand into the middle of the table, sparkling diamond solitaire front and center for everyone to "ooh and ahh" over.

"Congratulations," Walker tells her. As expected, I ogle her ring and try to ignore the stab to the heart it gives me.

"How about you, Diana?" Walker asks her when we're finally done congratulating a woman over the grand achievement in life of having a man ask her to marry him. I know, sarcasm is not attractive. It's just disgusting to me how Walker asks what they do and she answers with her wedding. Like that's something "to do" in the world that benefits society in any way.

"Oh, I'm a working girl. I'm a personal shopper at Barney's." Diana shrugs like it's no big deal, when in fact, I know it's her identity and she talks about her rich and famous clients constantly. Like a connection to powerful people makes her powerful by association.

The server saves this awkward conversation and we order, the girls deciding to split a bottle of wine between them. Walker and I stick to water, which I think is smart if we want to continue to pull off this fake relationship.

"So, how long are you going to keep cleaning up vomit, Jay?" Amy asks after our dinner arrives. I stop chewing and feel my shoulders creeping up toward my ears like they do when I'm stressed, but Amy continues to take a bite of her kale salad, oblivious to my distress. From the side of my eye, I see Walker clench his jaw. It's not his place to tell off my friends, but I can tell he's having to hold back from jumping in.

"I'm not sure you understand what a P.A. is, Amy. She acts as a doctor, helping young cancer patients fight for their lives."

I stiffen at Walker's defense of my profession, but he reaches over and places his hand on my thigh, effectively distracting me.

Amy's eyes widen. "Oh, I know that, Walker. Jemma and I just tease each other like that, don't we, Jay?" I don't respond and Amy keeps talking like the question was rhetorical. "It was just a little joke between friends." She beams at Walker and I've never wanted to eviscerate a person where they stand like I do right now.

"Uh huh." Walker stares at her, openly hostile. I sit back and will myself to relax. I lay may hand over Walker's and squeeze, trying to communicate that I'm fine. He can stand down now.

I clear my throat and set down my fork. "I don't know that I find that joke very funny anymore, Amy."

Amy stills, her expression clearing to that of an innocent girl, chastised for no reason. "I'm so sorry, Jay. I won't ever say it again."

"Thank you, Amy." I smile and go back to eating, ignoring the way Diana and Justine are watching us with wide eyes and zipped lips.

The rest of dinner has an awkward, forced element to it, but all the while, Walker and I lean into each other. Hold hands. Find reasons to touch. It's both soothing and stimulating, helping me to get through this ridiculous dinner. The resistance I had to texting him earlier is gone. The Walker from the cab is back, celebrity-Walker nowhere to be found.

We finish dinner and the girls stand to leave, inviting us to some club with them, but we both decline, saying we want an early night. Walker waggles his eyebrows at that and the girls leave in a bustle of giggling and innuendo.

We wait until they're gone before calling our own ride. Once we put on our jackets and hustle to the car, I breathe a sigh of relief.

"Thank goodness that's over!"

Walker chuckles. "And you didn't have one spaz moment the whole evening. Absolute success, don't you think?"

I laugh, loving that he doesn't mind my moments of complete craziness when the worst that could happen, often does. "True. I was so focused on our charade that I didn't get nervous and knock things over or trip over nothing."

Walker sobers quickly. "Are they always like that?"

I tilt my head back and forth. "Yes and no. It wasn't always like that, but the last few years have been." I take another deep breath. "I just can't keep doing that. I'm officially done."

Walker gives me a smile I can't define, I just know it warms my belly and feels a little like my second-grade teacher giving me a gold star sticker.

He grabs my hand and holds it, the gesture familiar now. His eyes seek me out in the darkness of the back seat. "High school is long over, Jemma. Whatever you feel you owe them has long since been paid. Besides, you have it all backwards. They're the lucky ones for having your friendship for so long. Not the other way around."

His words fill me up, making my eyes mist over. "Thank you, Walker," I whisper.

We hold hands in silence for a few minutes while I collect myself.

I huff out a laugh, the tears no longer threatening to fall. "You sure did a good job in there, boyfriend."

He looks down at our hands, his face in the shadows and unreadable. "I don't know how much of that was—"

He stops abruptly as the car turns into the drive of our hotel. I crane my neck and see a few people standing right outside the automatic doors, but no other reason for Walker to have cut himself off.

The car stops at the curb and before I can question him, Walker disentangles our hands and hops out. I scoot over and get out, careful to keep my skirt from flying up and my heels from sliding on the wet pavement. Walker glances back at me, but doesn't offer a helping hand. Instead, he walks off toward the entrance to the hotel, leaving me behind. He shakes hands with the people outside the hotel and then goes inside, completely unconcerned that he's left me out in the cold night air to fend for myself.

That sinking feeling is back, this time full force. I have no idea who Walker is: the guy at dinner whose eyes light up debating with me and holds my hand in support when I need it most or the jerk that walks away like none of that meant anything.

Logically, I know we're just pretending to be dating, but I've never felt more alive and aware of the things I ultimately want in life than when I'm with him. He's either the best actor I know or something's very wrong with him. Hot and cold, much? Either way, I can't keep letting myself get hurt like that. I refuse to even pretend to be with a man that would act like a different person around other people. Like I'm not good enough to even be seen with. Please. If I needed that judgement, I'd call my mother.

I slip into my hotel room, inhaling the cigarette stench, finding it more favorable than more time spent in Walker's presence and all his woodsy cologne deliciousness. As I get undressed and put on my pajamas, my mind is made up.

No more texting.

No more pretend boyfriend.

No more Walker.

I'll handle the rest of the weekend on my own. I don't need him to fight my battles. I'll face my friends head-on and do what I need to do. I'm glad he forced me to look at the issue and make a decision, but his help is no longer needed or wanted. If they wonder where he went, I'm sure I can come up with believable excuses.

I just spent the night pretending he was my boyfriend. I'm sure I can pretend his absence doesn't bother me.

alker

I tossed and turned all night, thoughts of Jemma twisting bizarrely with nightmares I'd had for years after my late wife passed away. In every nightmare, I was responsible for Jemma's injury or death, not by my hand, but because I'd walked away and let harm come to her.

It didn't take a psychologist to tell me what my dreams meant.

I felt guilty for ditching her last night.

In my defense, I'd been blindsided by the attendees standing outside the hotel when our Uber pulled up. I told Jemma right from the start I couldn't be seen with her at the hotel. For that very reason. The attendees at the conference would be milling about and I couldn't be seen wooing a gorgeous woman. They'd never take my speech seriously if they saw me off gallivanting with a woman like my late wife meant nothing.

Added onto my guilt about ditching Jemma so abruptly was

my guilt about so thoroughly enjoying my evening with another woman. Yes, our vows were till death do us part. And death had parted us, no doubt about it. But it had been so easy to think I'd moved on when in fact, I hadn't even been on more than a first date with a woman since my wife died.

I'd never memorized the way a woman's skin felt like silk. Or how she bit her lip when she was confused or thinking hard about something. Or the hours, days, months, years I could spend worshiping her mouth and the way she kissed me back.

And now that I feel all that and more, I have so much more I want to explore. I'm fascinated with the human heart. Not the parts that pump blood and keep us alive biologically. I'll leave that to the doctors in the world. I'm fascinated by the emotions of the heart.

How a heart could be completely shattered, yet still continue on. How it could be pieced together, whole, yet different. Tender, but hopeful. Then flushed with a tidal wave of love and affection without bursting at the seams so newly mended.

Part of why I blog about my grief is so I can understand it. Yet, I haven't explored this part of moving on and finding love again.

Not that I love Jemma.

It's way too early to even think about that. But just the possibility of having feelings again in this tattered heart of mine is novel and strange and wonderful.

So I get up before the sun and down two cups of coffee while I sit with my thoughts. It isn't so much meditation today but mulling over my discovery.

I glance at my watch and see I'll be late for my presentation if I don't get moving. Finishing my protein bar, I slide into my suit jacket and check my hair in the mirror. Then I grab my phone and key card and rush out the door.

Down in the ballroom, I enter quietly through the back and walk up the side of the room. The moderator finishes up whatever he was saying and then moves into introducing me. I wait for him to get through the familiar bio I wrote years ago and just update as necessary.

Then it's my turn and I leap onto the stage and adjust the microphone to my height.

"Thank you, Frank, for that warm welcome. Though I talked to most of you last night at the reception, I'd like to address some of your questions. Because at the end of the day, though the details will be different for each of us, we all share one common thing: our loved one has died. Wherever you may be in the grieving process, I have a message for you today."

I continue on with my normal spiel, the slides behind me changing when I click the button on the small remote in my hand. I'd know this presentation in my sleep, I've given it so many times. Public speaking comes naturally to me and I'm lucky I've been told I'm good at it.

So, when I get to the second to the last slide, I pause. And not where I'm supposed to.

I pause because it hits me that the presentation is really only half done. I'm missing the second half. The half where I talk about truly moving on and what that looks like and how it feels. For the first time ever, I feel like I'm letting my audience down.

I boxed myself into this role of talking about the first few stages of grief to the point I've stayed in the same place.

And nothing's more confining than realizing the box exists.

I end my speech like I rehearsed and walk off the stage to applause I don't deserve. I have my work cut out for me. I'm going to talk to Jemma and explore how I feel about her. And then I'm going to go home and finish that speech.

The organizer of the event shakes my hand as I pass by, his hearty handshake telling me he's happy with my contribution. I have to bite my lip to stop the word vomit that threatens to spill out. If he thought that speech was great, he'd love what I plan to present next time. Or maybe he'd hate it. Time would tell.

I pour a glass of water from the table at the back and sit in an empty chair off to the side. Other speeches are going on, but I don't hear them. My brain is whirling and at the forefront of all the chaos is a singular thought: I need to make things right with Jemma.

Walking off without her last night was rude. Plain and simple. No excuses. I freaked out and thought about my reputation before I thought about her feelings. My own fears over moving on led me to hurt another person, which is never okay in my book.

My thoughts stray back to the kiss, like the nightly cigar you just can't give up. You know it's not good for you, and even though you promise yourself every morning to give it up, come night-time, you're holding her in your hand and drawing her in.

The fact that the kiss cemented itself in the top position of best kiss of my life sends my heart racing. Yes, it was the kind of kiss to make a man want more, but it also scares me to think I've made some sort of ranking in my head, where my late wife, the woman I thought was the love of my life, isn't in the top position.

So like the addict I've become, I pull out my phone and type out a quick text, hoping no one can see my screen.

Me: Got any plans tonight with your fake boyfriend?

My knee starts jumping up and down as I wait for a reply. No reply bubble appears so I shut my screen off and try to focus in on the current presenter. He's droning on and on about managing one's anger. The days where I felt intense anger over the unfairness of cancer choosing my wife's brain as a breeding ground seem so long ago. Like those days belong to another person.

Checking my screen again and not seeing a text, I stand and slip out the back door. I can't sit still any longer. I need to make things right. After the way I treated her last night, she may not text me back at all. Apologizing over text seems like the millennial way out so I wrack my brain for a better plan.

It's on my second lap of the hotel lobby that the perfect idea comes to mind. It's a long shot and she may think I'm crazy, but I have to do something to get her to talk to me. I have to apologize and make sure she doesn't think my callous treatment had anything to do with her. It was all me.

And this gesture should help pave the way to that apology.

emma

My winged eyeliner is like an omen for today: why even bother?

After my twentieth attempt, I wipe off the jagged line with a makeup remover cloth and settle for a minimalist look of mascara and foundation. My friends won't care anyway. To them, I'm just Jay, the tomboy they felt sorry for in high school and tried to mentor. A follower to prop them up. A charity case.

Walker was like a magnifying glass at dinner last night, highlighting all the ways my friends were disrespectful. Previously, I knew they were not so nice, but with Walker there to witness it all, I saw the truth of our relationship with startling clarity. They were nasty.

I just had to get through today and tomorrow and then I'd be done. I'd find a way to remove myself from their clutches. Fading into the background and then disappearing forever is my preferred method of extraction. Barring that, I'd have to put on my big girl panties and face the nastiness when I broke things off with them in plain terms. Either way, it's happening, I'm sure of it.

Throwing my purse over my shoulder, I head down to the lobby to meet them. We have plans to go shopping, then lunch, then head back to the hotel for happy hour. I'm not a shopper per se, but anything is preferable to staying in the hotel and possibly running into Walker.

After last night's disappearing act, I have no intentions of texting him again. He sent me a text this morning, but I've vowed to ignore it. I'll make all the excuses necessary to my friends, but I'm not including him in my weekend any longer. Fake boyfriend act is over.

Because here's the thing: last night opened my eyes to how terribly my so-called friends treat me. I'm going to do something about them because I respect myself. But when Walker ditched me at the hotel and walked away like he didn't even know me after blowing my mind with that kiss? He made me feel the same way my friends do. Maybe even worse. And I've learned my lesson. No more crappy people in my life.

Period.

Surprisingly, my friends don't mention a thing about dinner last night, or Walker correcting Amy. She's a little cooler than normal with me while we shop, but that's to be expected anyway. She's gotten progressively nastier each year. Shopping turns into the perfect distraction, possibly because this is their happy place. By the time we make it back to the hotel, I'm feeling like I can survive this weekend without permanent damage.

"I'm going to run to the restroom real quick." I place my one small shopping bag on an empty chair at the bar and head off to the ladies' room. When I come back, the rest of the girls are already seated with their huge shopping bags piled on top of mine at the end of their row. There's nowhere to sit.

"Uh, guys?" They swivel their heads to look at me blankly. I gesture to the bags. "You going to let me sit or what?"

"Oh, sorry!" Diana hops up and moves the bags to the floor with a giggle.

Nothing better than feeling like an afterthought.

I control the eye roll and have a seat.

"What can I get you, miss?" The bartender gives me a nice smile and the girls giggle, shamelessly trying to draw his attention. Did I mention they're all married or engaged?

"Just a glass of white wine, please. Oh, and an iced water."

"So, any ideas for my bachelorette party?" Justine takes a sip of her rum and Coke, her meaning clear. She wants us to be planning something epic for her.

Before I can censor myself like I usually do around them, I remember how one of my coworkers is a flamethrower. "What if we did a Vegas weekend and saw one of the acts? My coworker was telling me about this flame-throwing show called Up In Flames going on in Vegas right now. He said it's phenomenal."

"Flame throwing?" Amy's looking at me like I suggested we eat bugs.

"Yeah, you know, where they—" I swing my arm in a wide arc to demonstrate how they make huge flame circles and instead, I hit the glass of wine the bartender just placed on the bar, sending it spilling to the floor with a loud crash.

I lurch backward in a futile attempt to avoid the shower, then hop off my tall chair to grab the broken glass stem off the floor. The glass is lying in several pieces, having broken on contact with the tile floor. Everyone's stare is like a weight on my back as I try to fix the damage I caused.

"Oh my God! That better not have gotten on my new dress!" Amy squeals above me.

The bartender materializes crouched next to me with a thick white towel.

"Stay back. I don't want you to get cut." He sweeps the liquid and glass shards into his thick towel then looks up at me. "That was my bad. I shouldn't have placed the glass right by your arm."

Even though my face is on fire, I give him a small smile. "No, no. It was my fault. I shouldn't have been gesturing wildly like that. Thanks for helping me."

He smiles back, then stands and offers his hand to help me up.

"Jeez, Jay. Way to go full klutz-mode on us." Justine is smiling, like it's a joke, but there's nothing funny about it.

Suddenly, flames are licking up my spine and making my head feel like it'll blow. My embarrassment burns away to ash, not much different than the state of this friendship. Previously, I'd slink away and hope they forgot my awkwardness, but now I'm just plain mad. I don't deserve to be talked to that way. I've had enough.

My hands are on my hips and my mouth is moving before I realize what I'm doing. "You know what? Thanks so much for your concern. I didn't hurt myself, not that you asked." I roll my eyes and grab my purse. "I'm going upstairs to change. Have a nice evening."

Spinning on my heel, I march off to the elevators, not even seeing their gaping mouths in my wake.

Unbelievable.

I jab the elevator button and tap my toe while I wait. That waiter, a perfect stranger, treated me better than friends I've known for over ten years. If that's not a sign, I don't know what is. My plan was to survive this weekend and then break things off with them, but now I'm thinking I need to do it sooner than that.

The elevator opens and I climb on, pressing the button for my floor and delighting when the doors close and I'm officially on my own, away from those hellcats. Back in my room, I kick off my wedges as soon as I cross the doorway and groan when I flop back on the bed, feet elevated, soft mattress supporting my back like a hug from the heavens.

After a few long minutes of deep breathing, I open my eyes and realize I need to get some dinner or I'll be starving in the middle of the night. I sit up, intent on finding the room service menu and indulging in a juicy cheeseburger.

And that's when I see it.

An unfamiliar navy blue suitcase sitting in front of the built-in hotel desk, a cream envelope sitting on top. My eyes narrow and I look around, feeling like I'm no longer alone in my hotel room. I approach cautiously, finally snatching up the envelope and pulling out a single piece of card stock.

I'm sorry. I don't deserve it, but please give me a chance to apologize in person and explain. Walker

I inhale as much oxygen as my lungs can take before blowing it out in a rush. *That man.*

Now I'm tapping my foot for an entirely different reason. A bubble of hope expands in my chest and just like that I can't think of anything but Walker. His tall, lean physique, the dark hair gelled to a stylish mess, that smirk morphing into a blinding smile that makes my heart trip, the way his lips teased mine. I want one more chance to smell that cologne, to feel his heat when I get close.

So I do it.

I text him.

Me: *Thank you for the new suitcase. Very thoughtful.*

I've barely hit send and I see a bubble pop up, showing me he's already texting back.

Walker: *Can I buy you dinner downstairs at the steak house in the lobby?*

I put the phone down and pace my room. I'm conflicted, but ultimately, I have to see him. He said he'd explain and there's part of me that badly wants to understand how he can go from warm and flirty to cold and distant in a split second. I can get my answer tonight and then walk away with closure.

Darting back to my phone, I tap out a reply before I can re-think it.

Me: *Sure. Right now?*

Walker: Yes! See you soon. ;)

Gah! Him and that winky face.

Sitting on the bed, I slip my wedges back on, promising my protesting feet that I'll give them a break tomorrow. There's a particularly pretty red silk blouse I brought but didn't think I'd have the special occasion to wear. Meeting Walker for a dinner date certainly qualifies and I'm ridiculously glad I brought it with me on this trip. I put it on, change my jewelry, brush my hair, touch up my lipstick, and I'm finally ready to go.

On the elevator ride back down to the lobby level, I cross my fingers I won't see my friends. I don't want to deal with them right now. I can only focus on one thing at a time and right now, all my focus is on Walker.

The doors swish open and I see him across the lobby, his tall, commanding figure hard to miss even with plenty of people milling about. My heart leaps despite telling myself I can't have him. This whole dating thing is supposed to be temporary anyway. Developing feelings for a fake boyfriend when he's acting hot and cold would be reckless. I'm never reckless. Clumsy yes, but not reckless on purpose.

I take several steps forward to greet him, my face splitting with a smile as I take in how smart he looks in a suit jacket and observe his handsome face searching the lobby for me. Then everything slows down, each frame happening in slow motion.

His attention is drawn to my left, his eyebrows coming together in a frown. I follow his gaze and see my three friends exiting the bar, heading straight for him. My heart dives down to my shoes. Amy flicks her long blonde hair behind her shoulder and smiles at him. I know that look. It's the same look a fox gives his prey right before he tricks them.

I'm attempting to approach, feeling like I'm walking through mud to get to him before they do. Still twenty feet away, I see them surround Walker, Amy in front. Her hand snakes up his chest to grab onto his lapel and I want to puke. She shifts not-sosubtly, pressing her body into his like the brazen, little hussy she is.

The flames from earlier reignite, this time raging high enough to burn down everything in my path. How dare they flirt with my pretend boyfriend? As far as they know, he's the love of my life. A good friend would never cross that line and flirt with her best friend's boyfriend. Ever. It's in the girl code.

My vision narrows to just him and her, the rest of the world a red haze I can't be bothered with right now.

Five feet away.

Walker swats her hand off his chest and tries to take a step back, bumping into Justine who giggles, the sound echoing in my head, mocking me with my choice of friends. His head lifts when I'm two steps away, his look of relief telling me all I need to know.

He steps to the side and grabs my hand, diverting me from the pack, my momentum keeping us moving together in stride.

"There you are, love. Let's get some food, huh?" He walks with me in the direction of the restaurant, but not before I look behind me and give the death glare to my ex-friends. Amy looks bored, Justine is still giggling, and Diana looks shocked by the turn of events. At least one of them gets the gravity of the situation.

Walker tugs on my arm and spins me around so I can't see them any longer. Then a warm hand is cupping my face. Before I can bank the fire that still rages, his lips are on mine, the anger quickly turning to passion.

His teeth nip at my bottom lip, demanding my attention though it's already his. My hands find purchase on the sides of his suit jacket, pulling him into me and hanging on for the ride. His palm tilts my head to the side and he dives in, consuming me with a kiss far more intense than last night, yet every bit as delicious.

11

alker

The fire in her eyes, the fierceness in her gait, and that lush bottom lip are too much for a mere mortal like me. Before she can light into her so-called friends, I grab her hand and march her away. And I know she thinks I'm only kissing her to give her friends a show, that's not at all what's going on here.

I can't keep my hands off her. Can't deny that I'm attracted to her, that she means something to me, that the heart once crushed is now beating again. For her.

So I take advantage of the situation and kiss her the way I never knew I'd want to again. She melts into me, that steel spine bending for me, a surrender I don't take lightly. I'm so damn lucky she gave me another chance after I treated her as badly as her friends over there.

Then my brain takes a back seat and all I know is this woman in my arms and her taste on my lips. A loudly clearing throat directly behind me is the only thing to pierce this fog around us.

With regret pulsing through every cell of my body, I pull away and stare into her hooded eyes. Satisfaction swoops through, seeing her eyes unfocused and soft.

"Excuse me, did you want a table?" A woman's voice from behind me forces my gaze to leave the heaven before me and see where we are, which is apparently the hostess station in front of the steak house.

"Um..." I look back at Jemma, her cheeks pink, eyes still hazy, and the last thing I want to do is be a table away from her with constant interruptions by a well-meaning server. "No. Thank you."

I slip my hand into hers again, tipping my head to the door off to the side, leading to what looks like an outside area. She gives me a sweet smile in response and I take that as permission, walking quickly to escape this hotel and everyone in it. I just need time alone with Jemma to explain my behavior, beg her forgiveness, and hope she's on the same page as I am. There's nothing fake about this relationship any longer.

The door clangs shut behind us and the quiet is a breath of fresh air. Jemma leans against the wall like her knees aren't holding her upright as they should. Her hair is tousled from my hand raking through it. Clenching my fists, I promise myself more kisses later if I can just say the things that need to be said.

"Jemma." Her gaze meets mine and I wonder if I could just stare at her forever, staying lost in her blue eyes. I clear my throat and begin again. "I'm so sorry for walking away from you last night. Dinner was incredible and leaving you was the last thing I wanted to do. But, truth be told, I freaked out. I saw some attendees from the conference outside the hotel and I felt like I couldn't be seen with you."

She frowns, but nods her head at me to continue.

"You see, I've created an entire brand around the fact that I'm a widower. It started out with my blog, where I poured my heart out online as it was breaking. Then came the book deal. And then the speaking gigs. People going through hard times look up to me as someone who understands them and can help them through it. If suddenly I'm gallivanting around with a beautiful woman looking like the happiest man alive, how does that affect them?"

I let the question hang in the air between us, because frankly, I don't have the answer to that. How can I bridge that gap and keep my followers with me? How can I show them happiness is possible in their future too without alienating them during their darkest hour?

"I guess I didn't realize you had this following you speak of. We really just met a little over a day ago. There's so much we don't know about each other." Jemma puts her hand on my arm and I know any backlash is worth a chance with her.

"I thought my ability to open myself to a relationship had died with my wife. And then I saw you and your hideous suitcase dragging through LAX."

She huffs out a laugh. I smile right back. "What I'm saying is that I'm into you, Jemma. I don't want to pretend to be your boyfriend to get your friends off your back. I don't want to hide you away so my audience is placated. I want to date you for real. I want to know what makes you laugh so hard tears stream down your cheeks. I want to know your deepest fears and celebrate your every success. I want to debate the downfalls of entitlement and snap judgements and all manner of topics with you. Please tell me you feel the same way?"

I'm gulping for breath when I get done. Who needs air when you're begging for a woman to give you a second chance?

Her grip on my forearm tightens, and a hesitant smile graces her face. "I don't know how any woman could say no to that speech, Walker. You really are a good speaker, aren't you?"

I bark out a laugh and then sober quickly. "My feelings for you are not fake, and that speech was not rehearsed. I promise you."

She nods. "I believe you. I won't lie to you and say there aren't genuine feelings on my end." Her gaze darts away and then comes back to me. "But I can also tell you that I'm smart enough to be cautious. I've let people treat me badly before and I've recently had my eyes opened to not putting up with that." She squeezes my arm again, her implication clear. "So, let's go slow and see. Okay?"

I take a step closer, her bright blouse blowing gently against me in the evening breeze. Still not close enough. "May I?"

Her eyes sparkle up at me, her head tilted back. "Oh, we're asking now, huh?"

"It's our first kiss, so yeah, I'm asking permission."

A line forms between her eyebrows. "Um, first kiss? Pretty sure we've had a couple already."

I shake my head, getting closer. So close I can see the light freckles across her nose that makeup can't hide. I push a lock of hair behind her shoulder. "Nope. Those were with an audience, when we still said we were faking this relationship. This, right now, is our first kiss."

Closing the distance, I sweep my mouth across hers lightly, still wanting that permission. Her lips part and I take it for what it is: a green light. I dive in, delighting in her breathy moans, the greedy way she grabs my suit jacket in her fists. Pulling her into me completely, I spin us around, slamming my own back against the wall, careful to never lose contact with her lips. I want to consume her until she agrees to love me forever, which even I know is way too soon, so I give her the space to step back at any time.

I don't trust myself, too overcome with a raging river of emotion crashing through my body to trust my actions. I never imagined I'd be here again, so lost in her, I don't know what to do or how to proceed. All I know is I want this. Maybe even forever. I've gone from frozen in my emotions to red hot, feeling everything all at once. It's a lot to take in.

A bright light pierces my consciousness, the back of my brain trying to get my body to step back and assess. Then a guitar runs through chords at a decibel only possible with big speakers. The screech of a microphone finally pulls us both away, Jemma stepping back and whipping around.

Unfortunately, neither one of us can tell what's going on since a spotlight is pointed in our direction, blinding us. I look left and see a small stage with people and instruments. A flood of people enter the open garden area from the other side, and that's when I see the tall tables scattered around and the band starts playing in earnest.

It's a reception. And Jemma and I are at the front of it.

And now everyone's craning their necks, trying to see who's standing by the stage and why we're in the spotlight. I raise my arm to block the light, which provides me with a glimpse of the conference organizer who shook my hand so heartily just this morning. Judging by his shocked expression, he saw us a few moments earlier when we were lip-locked.

Guilt immediately slams into me. I want to hide, run away, deny everything. At that thought I'm also bombarded with a hefty dose of self-loathing I've never felt before.

"Walker." Jemma tugs on my arm, trying to pull us back. We should at least get out of the ring of light aimed at the band. I know this, yet here I stay, stunned how easy a lie can get out of hand.

I look over at Jemma to register the concern on her face. She's gone pale and I want to hide her away to protect her, but I don't have that luxury right now. "I gotta say something."

Her head jerks in a semblance of a nod even as she backs away from me. "Okay."

"Stay here, don't leave. Okay?" She can't leave me now. This isn't how I wanted to do this, but now that it's out there, I have to address it.

Another head jerk, her eyes round with fright. I don't have confidence in her answer, but I have to make the leap.

I turn from her and hop up on the stage. The band comes to a halt in the middle of a song, surprised to see me there, but recovering quickly as they realize the crowd is distracted by something. That something is me.

A microphone is front and center, just waiting for me to take it and speak my truth. For someone who's bared their innermost feelings journal style in an online blog for the world to read, this is a thousand times harder. Maybe because I'm scrambling to keep up with the changes myself.

"Ladies and gentlemen, I only had one speech prepared for you this weekend, but I think I have a few more things to say if you'll indulge me."

There's some muttering in the audience but the crowd moves closer to the stage, interested in what I have to say. No one has thrown food at me yet, so there's that. I clear my throat and continue, trying to keep looking out at the audience but also trying to keep an eye on Jemma's whereabouts. She's off to the side, out of the light, looking like she wants to run away, but thankfully hasn't.

I look back out at the crowd and take a deep breath. "I've done you a disservice."

12

emma

I have no idea what's going on, but I'm still over here trying to process what Walker just told me before the bright light blinded us. I'm in awe he said he's into me and wants to date for real. Let me tell you, the single, lonely woman inside of me is jumping up and down squealing at a decibel that causes severe headaches. The more sensible, plan-things-out-at-all-costs side of me is flashing around a large, red stop sign, trying to be the voice of reason amidst all the squealing.

Now Walker's up on a stage, addressing the mass of people scattered across the lawn. I'm still trying to wrap my head around Walker being a semi-celebrity and whether that's something I want in my life. Him jumping up on a stage the minute after he professes to have feelings for me is rubbing me the wrong way.

All the warmth I felt in his embrace, all the passion he showed me in the kiss, has grown cold. My mind is all over the place trying to catch up to everything happening. One minute I'm about to do bodily harm to Amy, then I'm being kissed out of my mind, and then Walker's got a microphone in his face in front of a hundred people. What I really need to do is focus on what Walker's saying so I don't fall further behind.

"...know all about the death of my late wife and how I was able to process all that grief. But I left out a huge component. Because I just didn't know. Moving on and beginning to date again isn't something I've experienced and therefore couldn't talk to you about. Then that beautiful blonde over there"—Walker gestures to me and I freeze, feeling too many pairs of eyes on me —"swooped in with her broken suitcase and animated conversations."

He pauses and stares at me. Something about his hot gaze pulls me in and makes me forget about everyone watching, like he's now talking just to me. "I don't know how things will turn out or where we're headed, but I do know I want to find out. Melissa died. And it was tragic and she changed my life forever. But I didn't die." He looks back out at the crowd. "I have a whole life to live and part of honoring her is starting to feel again, like she'd want me to. I'm ready."

Walker places the microphone back in the stand and walks toward me, hopping down and pulling me with him. A smattering of applause comes from the crowd, but Walker doesn't seem to hear it or care about their reaction. Instead, he tightens his grip on my hand and leads me back into the hotel and into a small, empty ballroom adjacent to the lobby.

I'm out of breath, both nervous and excited. I've never had someone profess to have feelings for me in front of a crowd, in the spotlight and over the loud speaker. It's overwhelming, but then again, everything's been overwhelming since Walker helped me with my suitcase yesterday. I think that's just his style, his way of confronting life.

His kiss is bold too, the one he gives me the second the ballroom door shuts and we're finally, blessedly alone. I attempt to reach up and thread my fingers through his thick hair, but I'm pulled back. Breaking away from him, I look down and see the flowy sleeve of my blouse is caught in the door.

Way to ruin a perfectly romantic kiss.

Walker chuckles and opens the door enough that I can pull my blouse free.

"I'm going to have to watch out for you. You wind up in some interesting situations." Walker's smiling at me like I'm adorable, his eyes soft and teasing.

I quirk an eyebrow. "You sure you want to date someone with a propensity for mishaps?"

His eyes turn fierce, the chocolate brown irises turning a deep mahogany. His voice comes out in a rough whisper, setting off a shiver up my spine. "I don't want to date 'someone.' I want to date *you*."

That's all it takes for me to melt against him, my blouse cooperating this time, allowing my arms to pull him close and get back to that kiss. He has no objections either, the magic of his lips spinning time and making me forget everything.

A loud chirp interrupts what could have been mere minutes or hours later, time well spent in Walker's arms.

He pulls back and searches his pockets. "I'm sorry," he mutters.

"It's okay." My voice comes out surprisingly breathless.

I see the screen of his cell phone lit with an incoming call from someone named Ash. My stomach clenches at the thought of a woman calling Walker. There's no time to ask as Walker puts the phone to his ear and barks out a greeting. He's still just inches from me, staring into my eyes while he listens to whomever called him. The voice coming out of the phone, though it sounds like it's coming out of a metal tunnel, is decidedly male. My stomach unclenches and I instantly worry I'm in too deep, too soon to be reacting like that.

"Uh huh. Yeah, I know." Walker is nodding, a slight frown telling me he doesn't like what this Ash guy is saying. "No, I think it was well received."

Ash squawks at him for quite some time, during which I'm getting uncomfortable, like there's business Walker needs to attend to that I'm holding him back from. When I try to slip by him to give him space to talk, Walker tugs me back with a quick shake of his head.

"Okay, we'll come up with a plan." Pause. "I'm not sure yet. Let me check in with Jemma and then I'll let you know." He hangs up and frowns at the phone a second before putting it back in his pants pocket.

"Well, that didn't take long," Walker mumbles before turning up the wattage of his smile, like everything is fine.

He goes to cup my face, his eyes focused back on my lips, but I rear back, putting a hand on his chest to keep him in focus. "Don't brush it off. Tell me what's going on."

His smile falters and I can see the moment he decides to let me in. "That was my agent, Asher. He heard about my little speech a few minutes ago. Wants to know what's going on. Thinks I should issue a statement or something."

My hands go cold. "Wow, he heard about it that quick, huh? It's really that big of a deal?"

Walker cringes and I know I'm not going to like what he's about to say. "He actually suggests we hide our relationship for awhile. Kind of ease the public into the idea of me dating again."

My jaw goes slack. It's finally hitting me what a big deal this is. I mean, Walker must be a bigger celebrity than I thought if our kissing is that big of an issue. I definitely don't want to hide our relationship, like it's somehow shameful or wrong, but I don't want to hurt his career either.

"But don't worry, I told him that wasn't going to happen. There are other options." Walker rushes to assure me. He brushes a hair off my face and tucks it behind my ear. His simple touch starts to melt the ice block that has formed in my stomach because of his agent.

"Okay good. I'm not a fan of hiding." Hope fills me again. There's got to be a way for us to be together without tanking Walker's career. We just need to come up with a plan.

"Want to catch an early morning flight out of here? You can come back to my place and we'll discuss where to go from here?" Walker looks so hopeful, like he's scared I'll run away from all the complexities that come with dating him. And to be honest, I'm not all that sure things will work out, but I'm willing to try so I nod.

Walker's face transforms into a brilliant smile, those brown eyes warming by the second. He really is handsome, his height lending him an air of authority I'm finding irresistible.

"I have to be back at work on Monday, but there's no reason to stay here all day tomorrow. Let's get back home." I wrap my arms around his waist and tuck myself into his chest. He hugs me back, his big hands rubbing up and down my spine, making me feel wanted. Secure. Happy.

"I gotta call my friends and break up. That should be fun." I groan into his chest.

I feel his body shake before I hear his deep laugh. "I know you don't want the confrontation, but I know you'll feel one hundred percent better once you get it over with. And besides, I'll be right next to you, holding your hand while you do it."

Gah, he says all the right things.

"Thank you. That means a lot to me." I unlock my hands and force myself to take a step back. There were things to do first. "How about you call about switching our flights and I'll call Diana to let her know I'm leaving early?"

He studies my face for a moment and must see that I'm feeling confident. He nods and grabs his phone again. I do the same, tapping my foot and hoping Diana won't answer. After three rings I begin to feel like I'm home free.

"Jay? Where are you?" She sounds out of breath.

Crud.

"Hey, Diana. I just wanted to let you know that I'll be going home first thing in the morning. Will you tell the others?"

The noise in the background suddenly fades, like she stepped into a quiet room. "Why? I mean, I know you weren't too happy with Amy, but she was just joking, like she always does."

I sigh and pinch the bridge of my nose. "See, here's the thing. It's not teasing. The things she says to me are cruel. And I've let it slide for years. But I'm done now. I'm not saying we can't ever be friends, but I won't be hanging out with you guys unless I'm treated with respect."

Diana is quiet while my stomach is in knots. I hate confrontation.

"Seriously? We've been friends since high school, Jay." Diana sounds shocked and confused and a little bit angry.

"I know, which is why I didn't do this sooner. Every time I'm around you three, I end up feeling bad about myself. Good friends don't do that to each other. Even the fact that you call me 'Jay.' I told you guys years ago I hated that nickname, but you use it anyway. You make me feel like a third wheel, like you're doing me a favor by inviting me, and I'm finally over it."

"Is this because of Walker?" Diana still isn't getting it.

I throw my hand up in the air, even though she can't see me. "No! He encouraged me to do what I've already been thinking about doing, but that's it. This is about you guys treating me like crap. I'm done, okay?"

Diana sniffs. "Okay. I'm sorry to see you go. But don't think Amy will forgive you easily. Are you sure you want to do this?"

I sigh and shake my head. "Diana, this isn't high school anymore. I don't need to fear Amy's wrath or take her crap to make sure I stay in the 'club.' Tell Justine I'm sorry for bailing on her wedding, but I think it's best I don't attend. Maybe we'll talk later. Bye."

I hit "end" and feel the sudden need to sit down before my legs give out. Walker appears in front of me and pulls me into his chest, holding my weight, knowing what I need. He kisses my forehead and then finishes up his phone call with the airline.

"Good job, sweetheart. You were firm without being mean. You said what you needed to say. I'm proud of you," he whispers.

I sniff, feeling my eyes mist over with tears I really don't want to shed. "Thanks," I whisper back.

13

alker

Asher's phone call disturbed me more than I'd like to admit. As far as Jemma knows, we're heading home to work out a plan, something simple to release on my site so people understand what's going on. Ash ended the call urging me to keep it all a secret. I didn't want to emphasize his opinion with Jemma because I can already tell she's not sure about my celebrity status.

She immediately drew away from the stage and the spotlight last night. And I don't blame her. It takes some getting used to when perfect strangers make comments about your personal life and feel they have a right to know everything. I've had a few years to acclimate; she's just being introduced to it.

"Nice bag you got there." I wink at her, gesturing to the brand-new navy suitcase I had delivered to her room yesterday. We planned to meet in the lobby and head to the airport together after getting both our tickets changed to an early 8 a.m. flight.

She blushes and smiles up at me so sweetly she reconfirms my decision to be honest with the public about our relationship status. I can't hide her away; she's too innocent and beautiful. I want to shout to the world that we're a couple.

"Thank you again for the new bag. Although I think you just were looking out for other unsuspecting travelers who might fall victim to my exploding suitcase."

I laugh out loud at the memory of the duct tape holding her other one together, or how the handle pulled right off the bag. "Nah, I just didn't want to walk through the airport listening to those non-functioning wheels grind on the tile floor again."

She smacks my arm halfheartedly. "It was part of my charm. Got you to stop and talk to me, didn't it?"

I pull back, hand to my chest, acting shocked. "Why, Ms. Reed! Did you set me up? Was your bag just a ruse to draw in some naive widower who'd step in and sweep you off your feet?"

"Caught me," she deadpans and then bursts out laughing.

See? This is exactly why I have to get the public on my side. I want all these moments with her and I can't do that if we can only be seen together at certain times and only in private. Ash is wrong and as soon as I can get some time with him, I'll prove it.

Our flight is smooth sailing, and before I've had nearly enough time with Jemma, we're grabbing our bags off the baggage claim belt and sharing an Uber to my house in Newport Beach.

"So, where do you live?" I pull her hand into my lap in the back seat, needing her hand in mine. "I feel like we know each other so well, yet I know very little about you."

She squeezes my hand. "You know a lot of the deeper level stuff with me, but we haven't known each other long enough to go over the minor details. I live in Costa Mesa in a tiny home I just bought last year. It's not too far from work, which is great since I practically live there."

"Any roommates?"

"Nope, just me. The house is a total fixer-upper, and my mother gave me crap about buying it without a man around to help me, but I love it. Yeah, it needs work, but I just do a little at a time."

I shake my head slowly. "Where did I find you?"

"Duh, at the airport just a few days ago. Did you hit your head?" she teases me.

I reach over quickly and dig a finger in her ribs, prompting her to yelp. "Alright, funny lady. No. What I mean is, most women who live around me are too concerned about ruining their nails to do home improvements. It's refreshing to hear you like to do those kinds of projects."

She tilts her head. "Well, I truly believe anything worth having requires hard work. I don't expect things to be handed to me. I expect to get my hands dirty to get what I want." She shrugs. "Besides, working in a hospital with sick kiddos, you can't expect to have pretty nails and clean clothes for very long."

I literally feel it. The falling every poet has ever written about. I feel myself tumbling head over heels for her and there's nothing I can do to stop it. I don't want to stop this sweet slide into heaven. I've identified as a widower for so long, I'm awed that she's careened into my life. I'm stunned to have this opportunity to have another partner in life. Yes, logically, I know it's too soon to be speculating on our future or this relationship's longevity, but this feeling in my gut is telling me to pay attention. To make it work. That it's worth it.

Before I can answer her or share any of my inner musings, the car pulls up outside my house, a narrow but tall house right on the strand.

"We're here." I kiss the back of her hand, then deposit it back on her lap to exit the vehicle and get our bags out of the trunk. She gets out and cranes her neck left and right, taking in my neighborhood. I look around too, seeing it with new eyes.

"Wow, nice digs." It's a compliment, but somehow she says it in a way that doesn't sound complimentary.

I set our bags on the curb and slam the trunk closed. Tilting my head toward the side gate, I gesture for her to follow me inside. "When I finally started making some decent money, I only cared about one thing: finding peace. What's better for a broken heart than to stare at the ocean every morning and night while you contemplate life?"

My set of keys is buried in my bag. I dig for it while Jemma shifts nervously next to me.

"Lost your keys in your purse?" she asks me with a wink.

I sigh, full well knowing she's teasing me. "It's not a purse. It's a men's carry-all."

She pretends to sneeze yet still manages to say, "purse!"

I give her a wry smile and bring my keys out with a flourish, then open the door to my house. Shoving the bags inside the foyer, I grab her hand and pull her into me. "Welcome to my home."

She follows me inside and I give her the tour, ending at the main living room on the second floor. This is my favorite room and what sold me on the house. The entire back wall is a giant, floor-to-ceiling folding glass door with an unobstructed view of the Pacific Ocean. Right now it's deep blue, sparkling in the sunlight, with pelicans swooping by on a hunt for their mid-morning snack.

I take a huge breath, the calm coming over me instantly, like it always does when I view the water. I glance over at Jemma to see her staring at the waves, mesmerized. It's surreal to see her here in my home, taking in the same view that healed me.

"You said you're a blogger?" she finally asks, incredulously.

I huff out a laugh. "Funny when you put it that way. But blogging didn't buy this house. The blogging turned into a book deal, which turned into a second book deal, which turned into a speaking tour and sponsorships. The books and the speaking bought this house."

She blinks and finally looks away. "I don't know. Seems like lots of people blog and don't make a fortune from it. I think *you* were the deciding factor, Walker."

My chest expands with her praise. My head seems to increase in size seeing how she believes in me. I tug her closer and pull her into my arms. Her head fits right under my chin, her sweet-scented hair overwhelming my senses. I thought my view was complete before, but now I know it was missing Jemma. Because there's nothing more beautiful than her, standing in front of the window, the ocean her backdrop.

"Thank you for believing in me and what I do," I whisper to her. "That's why I want to work with Asher and get this right. I want to keep helping people, but I can only do that if they understand that opening themselves up to love again is part of the grief process."

She nods against my chest. "I get that, I really do. Let's call Asher and work it out, huh?"

Jemma pulls away from my body and I lean in to brush a quick kiss across her lips. The sooner we get this out of the way, the sooner I can be out and about in public with her and woo her the way I want to. Speaking of dating again, I need to come up with a plan there too. I haven't tried to sweep a woman off her feet in a long time. I feel rusty and Jemma deserves five-star wooing.

We move over to my huge leather couch and I get Asher on the phone. Putting it on the glass coffee table, I put it on speaker so Asher can meet Jemma.

"Hey, my man, Walker. Back in town?" Asher's voice booms out over the speakerphone.

"Just got back to my place. I got Jemma here with me on speakerphone. Jemma, this is my agent, Asher."

"Hi, Asher, lovely to meet you." Jemma smiles at the phone as if Ash can actually see her beautiful face.

"Likewise, Jemma." Ash clears his throat. "Well, my first thought was it would be better to hide this situation and slowly introduce Jemma. Kind of step her into the picture, if you will."

I interrupt him before he can go any further. "And you know that option is not acceptable."

To his credit, I don't hear exasperation in his voice. "Yes, fully aware. So, I think the only thing to do here is be completely upfront and as honest as possible. I think we release a statement on your website with how you met, where you're at emotionally, and not show any weakness. You're not asking for public approval to date Jemma, but you do want to use this as a way to help more people."

Jemma flinches. Something doesn't feel quite right with what he said. I pull at my collar. "I agree with being upfront and honest, but I'm not *using* my relationship with Jemma to do anything."

"Wrong choice of words. What I mean is that moving on and learning to open up to love again is part of what you can share with people. That's where you are on your journey, and since you've been so open and honest with people right from the start, it makes sense that you'd share this with them too."

Jemma nods but that smile of hers is absent. I really hope she isn't having second thoughts. I realize making our relationship a public spectacle isn't normal, but I'm hoping being with me is worth it.

"Okay, have Rachel write something up and I'll take a look." I need to end this call and get back to wooing my lady. If I'm not careful there won't even be a relationship to explain to the public.

"All right, talk soon, and nice to meet you, Jemma." Ash clicks off.

I reach over and pull Jemma closer. I need to be touching her right now, to know she's on the same page. "You okay with this plan?"

The hesitation is small, but there in the tiny pause before she answers. "Yes, I think being honest is always a good idea. But what do we do if the public doesn't react well? What then?"

And that's the exact question that's been in the back of my mind since last night. Am I willing to lose my career for Jemma?

14

emma

Monday is spent at work, my day filled with my beautiful sick kiddos, worried parents, prickly doctors, and coworkers who are closer friends than the women I spent the weekend with. The time in between patients, or when I'm filling in a chart, my mind is on Walker. He was so sweet to me last night, having spent the day together watching football and sharing all the details about our lives. Then today, he greeted me with a good morning text, bringing a smile to my face the instant I was up.

My heart feels like it's about to beat out of my chest whenever I think of him, which is often, but I also get an uneasy feeling in my stomach. When we talk about his celebrity status, he seems so different than me, as if we're talking about a different man, one I don't know. But then when we just hung out together, he seems perfect for me. A best friend who understands me.

By the time I make it home that night, I'm exhausted. My phone pings with another incoming text from Walker.

Walker: Check your email...Ash sent over the draft statement. Call me when you've read it?

Me: Will do. Off to soak in the bath.

Walker: Need me to wash your back?

Me: Nice try...

I shake my head with a giggle. It's a nice feeling to be wanted by a handsome man. I run some hot water in my tiny tub, my toes curling in anticipation of the heat working out the knots in my shoulders and neck while easing the ache in my feet. It wasn't easy being on your feet for ten hours a day. A lot of women my age were wearing step counters to make sure they kept active. Me? I was looking for ways to be less active.

My phone starts ringing and I immediately think it's Walker, probably calling to talk his way into coming over tonight. I answer with a smile, which ends in a groan.

"Jemma, is that you? Why did you ignore my texts?" my mother's voice blares across the phone.

"Hi, Mother. I just got home from work. You know I can't text you when I'm working."

"Yes, I know, but don't they give you a lunch break or something? I want to know if Justine was going to invite me to her wedding. Did you ask her?"

I roll my eyes so hard I give myself a headache. "No, Mother, I didn't ask Justine because even I'm not going to her wedding."

My mother gasps, like this is the worst news in the world. I've told her repeatedly about my issues with the girls and how badly they treat me. Some moms would encourage their daughters to seek out better quality friendships, but not mine. She thinks I should put up with their crap simply for an invite to their country clubs.

"What did you do?" she screeches.

"I stood up for myself and I appreciate your unwavering

support." My voice comes out hard, which is the only tone my mother listens to.

There's silence while I slip into my bath, lowering into the hot water with a soft moan. I lean my head back and get to the point so this call can be over with sooner and I can get to my bath in peace. "Besides, that's old news. I'm dating someone."

"What??" If I thought she screeched before, this one word takes things to a whole new level of shock.

"Yep, met him over the weekend and we're officially dating. I wanted to tell you before you heard about it."

"Wait. Back up. You just met him and you're already officially dating? That's not like you. And why would I hear about it? Do I know him?"

I use my toe to shut off the hot water, wondering how quickly I can get my mother off the phone. "Well, he's a bit of a celebrity in his space. He's a speaker and author for grieving widows and widowers."

She starts laughing, the sound growing in volume with each passing second.

"What's so funny, Mother?"

"My daughter. The one who only dates someone if he fits exact parameters of whatever the hell you're looking for, is dating a guy she just met. And he's a celebrity? Come on, Jemma. You have to see the irony in that. You *hate* celebrities. That's, like, your thing. Wanna get Jemma angry? Start talking about how wonderful some celebrity is."

She dissolves into laughter again and the unease in my stomach grows. She's right. On paper, Walker is all wrong for me. I can't talk about all that with my mother though. She'll just keep laughing and teasing me. I need to talk to someone who will actually listen to me and give me solid advice. Honestly, the first one to come to mind is Charlotte, the sweetheart who works at Java Point right by the hospital. I stop there every morning and most weekends. She works all the time and we've become friends.

She's the best listener I know, which is a sad state of affairs when the local barista is a better friend to me than my own mother or the friends I've known since high school.

"Okay, Mom, sorry to interrupt comedy hour, but I gotta go. I'll call you a bit later."

"Sorry, honey, it's just a shock, that's all. I love you."

Mhmm... "I love you too."

We hang up and blessed silence fills the air. Which is what I wanted, but now depressing thoughts are swirling through my head. Maybe I've gotten caught up in a whirlwind weekend away from home, thinking that kind of relationship can last here in the real world where I work crazy hours and Walker is some semi-celebrity with fans to consider.

I think back on when he talked to me about his late wife in the taxi. He'd seemed so sincere, so heartbroken. And I could relate, having been around cancer patients for years, witnessing the devastating news of that diagnosis. Maybe I got sucked into believing we had more in common than we actually did.

I stay in the bath until the water goes cold, debating my thoughts and feelings, almost resorting to making a pros and cons list like a RomCom movie gone cliché. Instead, I put my pajamas on and curl up in my bed with a book.

I'm two chapters in when my phone pings again.

Walker: Get a chance to read it? Want to make any changes?

Oh crud. I forgot to read the statement Asher sent over.

I click over to email and pull up the attachment. It's super short and to the point, merely stating that Walker and I have just started dating, with no implications as to what that means for our future or Walker's job. My stomach clenches though when I see my full name in black and white, my personal business about to be released to the public.

I don't know if I can do this.

As soon as the thought flutters through my brain, I feel guilty. Like I'm being weak for allowing some nameless person to dictate what I do in my personal life. I rub my forehead, feeling all that tension seeping back into my body, the bath being no match for my conflicted thoughts.

Me: Looks good. Still scary...

My phone rings, showing Walker's name on the display. I answer quickly, knowing this conversation needs to be on the phone, not text.

"Hey." My tone is subdued, just like my feelings at the moment.

"Sweetheart, we can't let this change anything. It's just a simple statement on my website and then we can carry on however we'd like. This doesn't change anything." His voice drops to a whisper. "Don't let it."

The back of my eyes burn, that whisper of his doing more to my insides than any typed-up statement. He's right. I can't wimp out now. I can't bring myself to say goodbye to him. Not yet. Not now.

"Okay," I whisper back.

"Good. Thank you, Jemma. Everything will be fine, you'll see." He lets out a sigh of relief and I feel a twinge of guilt for making him doubt me. "What else can I do to make sure you feel better about everything? Just tell me and I'll do it."

I lie back on my bed, letting my pillows swallow me up. "There's nothing you can do, Walker. You've been great. It's just I've had bad experiences with celebrities in the past through work. They've been irresponsible and left sick kids hanging when they should have been doing all they could to bring a smile to a kid with a limited number of days left on this green earth."

"Thank you for telling me. I can assure you I'm not like that. I take my responsibilities seriously. You can count on me, Jemma."

He sounds so earnest, I can't help but believe him. I have to trust him and see if my belief about celebrities is wrong.

I drop my voice, the words too solemn to speak full volume. "I can promise you I'll try to keep an open mind. I want this to work."

"That's all I ask. Just give me a chance."

The statement is posted on Walker's website the next day.

His social media accounts are immediately bombarded by a mix of well-wishers and disgruntled people who want him to wallow in his grief forever, just like them.

I break my cardinal rule at work and check my phone between patients, hoping for a text or call from Walker. When I don't get either, I resort to skimming the comments on his social media sites. Funny how the majority of encouraging comments get swept aside and forgotten by the nastiness of the others. If my stomach was in knots last night, it's even worse today in the face of the minority's anger and hurt.

I'm questioning whether we're doing the right thing. How can dating me be worth tanking Walker's whole career? Maybe if I actually cared for him I should step aside and let him get back to helping people, not upsetting everyone.

As I go home for the day and still haven't heard from Walker, I've convinced myself to just fade into the background and disappear from his life. He can't be thinking it's worth it. Maybe he feels badly too and can't bring himself to tell me.

I do care for Walker. Very much.

So I need to do the right thing and let him go.

15

alker

I've been bombarded with phone calls from Asher all day long with words he wants to tweak on my website that will magically calm the backlash. Photos have somehow surfaced from the reception at the conference in Denver, where Jemma looks like a deer in headlights behind me, my hand intimately on her hip. I've seen the nasty comments on my social media and want to respond but Ash keeps telling me not to. Then my publisher called with questions as to what was going on. We were in talks about book number three, but if the backlash didn't die down quick, I'm sure I wouldn't be receiving a contract for that book deal after all.

And through all the craziness of today, I'm actually shocked. I was completely oblivious to the fact that people care what I do with my personal life. Sharing all my personal thoughts along the journey of the grieving process always felt cathartic. It felt natural and normal to connect with others going through the same thing.

It even felt like the natural evolution of things to become a leader in helping others new to widowhood by way of my books and speaking gigs.

But today I've gotten my first taste of the flip side. Today is the first day I regret ever hitting publish on that first blog post. Somewhere along the way others' opinions of my choices began to matter in a very real way.

I'm angry. I want to tear my hair out. I want to rage at the unfairness of it all. I want to hold Jemma close and pretend we can hide out in our own little world.

I'm angry that I'm letting a small group of hurting people tear me down with their words. Hurt people, hurt people. I'm furious that Jemma will read these comments and be hurt by them. I'm upset that I've known such grief and sadness for so long and the first time I've opened myself up to being truly happy again, people are trying to hold me down. Like I signed up for a life sentence to wallow in my grief, never to escape.

My phone rings again and I want to throw it out the window. Taking a deep breath, I pick it up, thinking it has to be Ash again. What I see on the display makes me pause. It's my sister-in-law, Melissa's sister. I can only imagine she's seen the news and has some choice words for me too.

Could today get any worse?

"Hey, how are you?" I try for a pleasant, non-stressed, happy greeting.

"Walker, I'm surprised you picked up." Her voice is smooth, not overly upset which makes me wonder what this phone call is all about.

"When I see it's you calling, of course I pick up. What's going on?"

"Well, I've heard the news and I've got to admit, I'm surprised."

I start pacing my living room floor, the ocean view not soothing me as it usually does. I tug at the collar of my shirt, feeling hot even though it's a perfectly reasonable winter day at the beach. "That makes two of us. I'm sorry I didn't get a chance to tell you personally that I started dating again. It all happened quite quickly and my agent advised me to make a public statement as soon as possible before rumors took over."

There's a pause and I can't help but think she's winding up to batter me over the head. Melissa was her sister, after all. I don't expect her to take it well, knowing her beloved sister's husband has moved on.

"Oh, Walker." She sighs, her voice low and calm. "Of course it's a shock to think of you with anyone other than Melissa. But I also know it's been eight years since she left us. It's only natural that you'd move on at some point. In fact, I'm happy for you. I really am. I know Melissa would have wanted you to find happiness again." Her voice wobbles and I hear a telltale sniff over the line.

I squeeze my eyes shut and fight to stay above the tidal wave of guilt that tries to sweep me under. "I can promise you this doesn't mean I love Melissa any less. Or that I've forgotten about her. She was one of a kind."

A watery acknowledgement follows in the silence. She finally speaks and the hurt is tangible in her voice. "I know. Just make sure this Jemma woman makes you happy. That's all I ask. Make sure she's worth it."

There's not much to say after that so we exchange a few pleasantries and catch up briefly on each other's lives before saying goodbye. We share a grief so intimately, yet I can already feel a huge chasm between us with this new development in my life.

I finally sit down on my couch and hang my head. My shoulders feel like there's a ten-ton weight sitting on them. My phone pings several times in my hands and suddenly it's all too much. Flipping the switch to silent, I set my phone down on the coffee table and step outside to my patio.

It's time to do what I've always done when overwhelmed and

unsure what to do: meditation. I sit on a blanket and stare out at the ocean waves for quite some time before closing my eyes and drifting off to a place where death doesn't exist and public opinion doesn't matter in the slightest. A place where everything is calm.

∽

It's been two days since the news broke on my website. Two days since I've communicated with Jemma. Two days where I've waffled back and forth with how I want to proceed. Two days where I've wallowed in my indecision and grief and guilt.

I know my silence isn't fair to Jemma. She deserves to hear from me. And yet, I haven't heard from her either and in my current state of mind, I figure she's decided I'm not worth the effort. She's already shared with me that she doesn't have much regard for celebrities, and with the hubbub stirred up by a few angry people, she may have decided that dating me just isn't worth it. Quite frankly, I don't blame her at all.

Around dinnertime, my doorbell rings. I'm loath to answer it since I'm still in sweatpants and a t-shirt that's seen better days. I swipe a hand through my hair and hope for the best. Peering through the peephole, I see it's just Asher. I swing open the door and let him in.

"What's up, man?" We shake hands and bro-hug as he comes inside. He's a few inches shorter than me, but has more muscle. We've worked out a few times together, but he's a beast in the gym. I can't keep up with him. I tried to get him to do meditation with me one time. He was equally bad at that. Despite our differences, he's a great guy and I wouldn't want anyone else as my agent.

"Dude. When was the last time you showered?" His face is twisted into a grimace.

I lift my arm and sniff, laughing when I realize I stink. "Um, not sure?"

He shakes his head at me and flops down on the couch. "Just like I thought. You've been pretty silent since everything went down and I figured you were wallowing. Time to get up, get cleaned up, and get on with your life. Go ahead. I'll wait here for you."

He waves me off, telling me what to do in my own house. "Hey. Go do whatever it is you do as an agent. I'm fine right here." I flop down on the other end of the couch and slouch down, getting comfortable.

A giant sigh escapes before he leans toward me. "Okay, listen. There were a few small-minded people who don't want you to ever be happy because that will shine a light on how unhappy they are. And they can't handle that realization. So...what? You gonna let them influence what you do with your life? That's lame, man. I can't let you wuss out like that."

I shake my head. "You don't get it. Yes, their comments bothered me, but more than that, Jemma hasn't even tried to contact me. She doesn't want to bother with all this just to date me. So this whole thing? It's been for nothing." That painful truth burns between my ribs. I'm hurt that Jemma doesn't think I'm worth a little public disgruntlement.

Ash cranes his neck left then right, looking for what, I have no idea. Then he drills me with his gaze. "Where did my friend Walker go? Because this pathetic man in front of me isn't him."

Ouch.

"I don't see you lifting a finger to go get your girl. Maybe she's waiting for you to call her. Maybe she thinks you don't think *she's* worth it. You want to be happy? Go out there and grab it with both hands and don't let go! I'll say it one last time. Get up. Get cleaned up. And then go prove to Jemma you're worth it."

He pops up and motions like he's dropping the imaginary

microphone before spinning and walking out of my house without another word.

I blink a few times, his words spinning through my head. Could he be right? Was I sitting back and letting life happen to me without making an effort to go get what I want? Because I'm pretty sure I want Jemma. Public approval or not.

I want to hear all about her day and her precious patients. I want to travel with her. I want to meditate with her on my balcony. I want to hold her hand and help her up when she inevitably stumbles over something. I want to share my tattered heart with her because I know she'll take good care of it. I want to be the reason she laughs more and stands up for herself more. I want to know her completely.

I love her.

A waft of my own stink hits me when I jump up from the couch with my realization.

I have to go take a shower.

And then it's time to plan out my grand gesture. Because it's going to take a really big one to prove to Jemma that I love her.

I'm worth it. She's worth it. We're worth it.

emma

It's funny how living on your own can feel so good for so long and then one day, a random interaction with a stranger can change all that. Ever since Walker swooped in and saved me from my suitcase, I crave the companionship that I only feel with him. And since he's gone silent? I feel a loneliness I've never experienced before.

My house is cold and dreary with only my own mess to show someone even lives here. My job no longer feels fulfilling without someone to share it with. My mind keeps craving a trip to the beach, but I know it's only so my heart can be near Walker.

I still check his social media accounts like a desperate woman, only to see no further posts from him, nor any ongoing nastiness from his following. And still, I haven't heard from him. My decision to disappear from his life is confirmed the longer I don't hear from him. Staying away is slowly killing me, but it's looking to be the right choice for his career.

Friday morning I pull on the first scrubs my hands find and sweep my hair back into a messy ponytail. Makeup and flat irons, I decide, are for women who aren't heartbroken. I skip my usual smoothie and stop by Java Point to see my friend Charlotte and grab breakfast.

The warm air blasts my face when I swing open the door to the coffee shop. I wait in line behind several men in suits on their way to work. I see Charlotte behind the huge machine churning out coffees that practically run this city. She catches my eye and winks. She knows my usual and will have it made by the time I get to the register to order and pay.

"Jemma, my love, how are you?" She slides my coffee and egg white sandwich to me across the counter and leans in to study me. Her accent is beautiful, though I can't place where she's from exactly and she's never divulged. She's a confusing blend of open and warm, mixed with secrets and deflection.

I shrug, the only answer I can muster at the moment.

Her eyes narrow and her gaze flicks over my straggly hair before she nods quickly. "Hold that question." She spins around and whispers to the guy next to her in the signature Java Point blue apron. He nods back and she ducks under the counter to come over to me. "Why don't we sit and chat on my break, huh?"

I let her pull me over to a small table in the back and slump in my chair. The first sip of the hot mocha she made for me permeates my funk. *At least something in this life is sweet right now.*

"Spill it, love." Charlotte leans over the table and gives me that sweet smile of hers that makes you cough up all your secrets. I don't know where she learned it, but I know its effectiveness firsthand.

I take another sip for courage, then launch into my tale, starting with meeting Walker at the airport, to our conversations, his announcement on stage, and then to his public posting of our relationship.

"And then...nothing. I haven't heard from him since Monday. And I think it's for the best. Clearly, being with me is going to tank his career, so it's best I stay away. Don't you think?" I finally wind down, picking up my sandwich while she digests everything I've dumped on her.

She folds her hands on the table and smiles at me patiently. "My sweet Jemma. You fell in love last weekend!"

I nearly choke on my sandwich. "No! I mean, I really like Walker, but we've only known each other a few days. You can't fall in love that quickly."

She shakes her head while her smile grows. "Yes, you most certainly can. And you did. True love is a precious thing. Why would you just walk away from that?"

I decide to drop the argument about falling in love. She can go ahead and believe that if she wants. "I'm walking away because it's what's best for Walker."

She throws her hands up. "Exactly! Because you love him."

I slump down in the chair and scrub my hands over my cheeks. "Argh! Maybe. I don't know. All I know is I feel horrible."

Charlotte nods. "I know, love. Why don't you go talk to him? You're assuming he doesn't want to be with you when you don't know that for sure. Be brave. Go find out. You barely even gave things a shot. If you quit now, I'll forever be disappointed with you."

My jaw nearly hits the table. "Wow, Charlotte, that's pretty harsh."

With a giggle, she stands up and leans down to hug me. "That's because you don't listen to subtle. Go get your man." She walks away without a backward glance, nor an apology I might add.

I shoot imaginary darts at her with my eyes while she gets back to work and ignores me. I finish my sandwich and take the rest of my mocha with me when I stand to leave. One last glance at Charlotte and I see she's eyeing me. One beautifully arched eyebrow rises, her lips pursed, and I know what that look means. She's daring me to actually do something about my heartache.

And sure enough, that tough love ignites some fire in my belly. The caffeine has cleared the cobwebs in my brain and now I'm thinking in terms of fighting for what I want. I didn't finally stand up to my lifelong friends for treating me like crap to let a man do the same thing.

I want answers. And by God, I'm going to get them.

There's some sort of commotion at the front entrance to the hospital so I go in the back way, swiping my card and jogging up the stairs, only tripping once but catching myself before I completely wipe out. I don't know what Charlotte put in that mocha, but I feel like I've had a complete turnaround this morning. I've got patients to see and time to formulate a plan to confront Walker. I want one last try to see if this will work between us. And if it won't? He needs to say that to my face like a man.

Yeah, baby. Look at me being all self-confident.

I barely skim the first chart at the nurses' desk on my floor when our head physician comes up next to me. Considering I don't normally see him out on the floor on a regular basis, I'm surprised to see him sit down next to me.

"Good morning." I give him a broad smile that he returns. I don't know that I've ever seen him smile before.

"Morning. Thanks for sending Mr. James our way. He'll be a great addition. You should get down to the press conference, don't you think?"

My nose just went numb at the mention of Walker's name. I'm so confused. What is he talking about?

"What?" I've completely forgotten about my charts. In my depression this week, did I forget something else?

"Mr. James? Downstairs? Go!" He stands up and walks away, shaking his head at my ignorance.

There's a weird rushing noise in my head. I think Charlotte put way too many shots of espresso in that coffee.

I stand up quickly, the chair rolling back and hitting the wall. There's no time to waste. If Walker's here, I need to find him. I know I wanted to have a plan together for approaching him, but him being here is an opportunity I can't waste.

When I reach the front lobby of the hospital, I see a small group of reporters standing around. My gaze rakes over the crowd until it lands on Walker, looking deliciously handsome in his blue suit and brown shoes standing with another good-looking man. I screech to a halt and drink him in. His hair is gelled back neatly and he's freshly shaven. I immediately regret my refusal of the flat iron before I left my house this morning.

Walker's head tips up and he sees me across the room, like he could feel my presence. He smiles and I can't help my smile in return. The tight fist clenching my stomach for a week now lessens its grip. He holds his hand out for me and I walk forward as if in a trance.

"There you are. I was waiting for you." When I reach him, he holds my hand and brings it to his lips, placing a sweet kiss against my skin and tugging directly on my heartstrings.

"Waiting for what?" My voice comes out breathy and I don't even care.

He winks. "You'll see."

He spins around and propels me forward in his normal way. Seems he's always grabbing my hand and bringing me along with him. I've missed that too.

He approaches the reporters and pulls me alongside him. When his arm is firmly around my waist he begins talking and the reporters begin taking notes and taking pictures.

"I asked you here today to get the word out about a new initiative Jemma Reed and I have put together. I've teamed up with the Hoag Pediatric Cancer Center to provide counseling classes and one-on-one support for families dealing with a loved one's cancer diagnosis. I've previously focused my work on widows and widowers, but we feel families could benefit from counseling at all stages of diagnosis. Please stay tuned for further information forthcoming about specific programs and when they will be launched. Thank you for coming."

I'm stunned. My heart is tripping over itself coming to terms with what he's offering. What he's already planned out. Would a man no longer interested in me be making plans to work with my hospital on a long-term basis? Would a man hiding me away from the press bring me here today in front of all these reporters?

Shouted questions are lobbed at Walker. He answers a few and passes off a few to his agent, Asher, the man I saw him standing with when I first entered the lobby. One particular question catches my attention and pulls me out of my thoughts.

"How do you respond to your followers who feel like you've abandoned them with the new announcement earlier this week?"

Walker's arm tightens around me and he opens his mouth to answer, but I stop him with a hand on his chest. "I got this one, if you don't mind." He nods, but his eyes are stormy.

I step forward and address the reporters for the first time. "Hello. I'm Jemma Reed. To answer your question, neither Walker nor I want to live our lives based on the reactions of others. Walker lost his wife eight years ago and will forever continue to grieve her loss. However, Walker did not lose his own life. He has as much right as anyone else to love again, however and whenever he deems appropriate for himself. We both regret that some aren't able to see that point of view, but we won't apologize for finding love in a world that could use so much more of it. Thank you."

When I step back, Walker pulls me into his side, nuzzling my ear. "Thank you," he whispers, sending shivers down my arms.

Asher takes over the last few questions of the press conference and Walker pulls me aside to an alcove off the lobby. His hands grip my upper arms, his face hopeful.

"Did you mean what you said? Did we find love?" His thumb brushes back and forth on my skin below the hem of my scrub top.

Time to get my man and make Charlotte proud. Time to make myself proud. I tug on the lapels of his suit jacket, bringing him closer.

"I know so."

The words are barely out of my mouth when Walker crushes me to him, his hands tugging my hair out of the ponytail.

"Thank God," he whispers. Then he's pulling me back so he can look into my eyes. "I love you, Jemma. I don't know how when we've only known each other for a few days, but there it is. I don't want to run from it or question it. I want to savor it and nurture it."

I can't swallow with the lump in my throat, the tears threatening to spill down my cheeks at his words. "I love you too. Even though I tried to stay away so you wouldn't lose your career over me."

He touches his forehead to mine still not breaking eye contact. "I don't care about my career if I can't have you, Jemma. You gotta know that."

I nod softly, accidentally dislodging his forehead from mine. A tear escapes and traces its way down my cheek, only to be caught and wiped away by his thumb.

"No tears, my love, just happiness. Let's wring all the happiness out of this life that we can."

A teary laugh burst out of my mouth. "How am I going to concentrate on work today after all this?"

His big hand covers my forehead. "You are feeling kind of feverish..."

The tears clear entirely now, leaving me feeling light on my feet. The heavy drag of uncertainty is finally gone. "Okay, mister. I'm not calling in sick." I poke him in the gut and he jumps back in surprise. "Want to come over tonight after I get off?"

He kisses me again, quickly this time. "Just try to keep me away."

EPILOGUE

alker

The ocean breeze comes off the water much differently way out in the Pacific. At home in Newport Beach, the breeze is chilly, even in the middle of summer. Here on Kauai, the wind is warm, the air scented with the native flowers that grow wild all over the island.

When I got the call to speak in Hawaii, I couldn't turn them down, even though my calendar has been packed the last few months. Ever since I announced my partnership with the Cancer Center, my publisher offered a huge book deal, the backlash from the announcement of my dating Jemma died down completely, and Asher's phone was ringing off the hook with speaking gigs for a much wider variety of audiences.

In fact, dating Jemma and opening myself up to new experiences has been the best thing for my career to date. But that's just my career. Dating Jemma has done amazing things to my heart, as well.

When Melissa and I were together, we'd been so young and blissfully in love. Naive, even, to the negative things that inevitably happen in life. I like to think our marriage would have weathered the test of time, but I'll never know for sure. What I do know is that loving Jemma is everything my thirty-four-year-old self needs.

She loves every part of me, even when I have moments of sadness or doubt. She understands that a tiny part of my heart will always belong to another woman. She's gracious, she's silly, and she's the most amazing woman I've ever met.

Which is why I have a diamond and platinum ring in my pocket right now, just waiting to be placed on her finger. She took some vacation time from work to come with me on this trip. Now that my speech is over, the next four days are ours to do with as we'd like. And I'd like nothing better than to make her my fianceé.

Jemma exits the bathroom in a little black dress and heels, her hair curled down her back. She gets a few blonde strands in her lipgloss and pulls them free before smiling at me and twirling so I can see her whole dress. I think back to that day at the airport when I saw her struggling with her suitcase. I had no idea I was meeting my future wife. Had no idea how happy my life was about to become.

"You look stunning, sweetheart." I kiss the back of her hand and then place it in the crook of my elbow while we stroll out the hotel room door to our reservations. The night air is balmy, the sound of the crashing waves quite loud given how close our room is to the ocean.

"You look quite dashing yourself, Mr. James— Oh!" Her hand tugs on my arm and I pull up to steady her. Her heel is caught in a crack in the sidewalk.

"Can't take you anywhere..." I mutter, then dodge her hand swiping at my head in response. I chuckle, even finding her clumsiness adorable. After crouching down and freeing her heel, we make our way to the hotel restaurant extended out over the water, white lights strung along the path to illuminate our way.

Once we get seated, the server immediately serves us champagne and then leaves. I called ahead and told the staff what my plans were for the evening. They were instrumental in getting everything to come together for my proposal.

"Wow, champagne the minute we sit down. This place really is a five-diamond restaurant." Jemma swivels in her chair to look around at the romantic setting. As for me, I can't seem to take my eyes off her.

I lift my glass and wait for her to follow suit. "To us, may we always be in love like we are tonight." We clink glasses and sip.

"You know, Mr. Professional Speaker. I don't think I agree with that toast." Jemma has a smirk on her face that makes me want to kiss her until she laughs it away.

I lift an eyebrow. "Well then, please, gift us with a better toast."

She smiles triumphantly and lifts her glass. "To us, may our love grow every single day for the rest of our lives." She clinks our glasses and I sip, nodding my head.

"Okay, fine. You're right, that was better." I put my glass down and stuff my hand into my pocket, fishing the ring out and holding it under the table.

Jemma puts down her glass and does a little shoulder shimmy in her chair. If I wasn't so nervous all of a sudden, I'd be laughing at her impromptu dance party in the middle of a fancy restaurant. I always love it when she does unexpected things that most women would be too self-conscious to do.

I swallow hard and go for it. "Speaking of the rest of our lives..." Jemma's gaze pops back up to my face and she smiles at me, tilting her head in question. I push back my chair and stand up, loving the way Jemma's eyes widen. I come around to her side of the table and then drop to one knee. Her jaw drops open and I hope the staff is getting some pictures like I asked. Her expression is everything.

Taking one of her hands in mine, I continue. "We've only been together for a short five months, but I've known since the first week. You're my forever. The one I want to live the rest of this life with, have a family with, the one I want to grow old with. I promise to be the man you want and need. I promise to never let you fall—even if you catch your heel or lose the wheels on your suitcase." Jemma's eyes fill with tears while a smile splits her face. "Promise you'll be my wife?"

She nods a couple of times. "Yes! Yes, I'll be your wife." Her arms come around my neck and we squeeze each other tight. I can feel her trembling, her tears turning to laughter in her excitement. My nerves are finally gone, now that she's said yes. My heart is still racing because I know I now have everything I've always wanted and for many years didn't think I'd ever have again.

We finally let go long enough for me to place the ring on her finger, both of our hands shaking.

"Oh! I didn't even see the ring." Jemma stares at it on her hand and then hugs me tight again. "It's so beautiful!"

I finally make it back to my seat and we order dinner. The staff brings us course after course, along with more champagne and a bouquet of flowers for Jemma. It's over dessert when the smile finally fades from her face.

"Walker?" That little frown line is back between her eyes.

I squeeze her hand on the table, suddenly concerned. "What is it?"

Her gaze finds mine and she pauses like she's reconsidering what she's going to say.

"You can tell me anything, sweetheart."

She nods and asks, "When we have our wedding, you know how the tradition is 'something old, something new, something borrowed, something blue'?"

I dip my head, urging her to keep going.

"Well, do you think I could make my 'something borrowed' something of Melissa's?"

I freeze.

"So, you know—she can be with us even now," Jemma rushes to explain. She finally stops talking and looks at me, her eyes troubled. I see her throat swallow slowly and I can only imagine what it took for her to ask me that question.

I can't even answer her I'm so blown away by the heart of this woman. I'm humbled. I'm awed that this paragon of a woman wants to be with me.

Melissa would love her.

My eyes fill with tears and Jemma's worried face wavers in front of me.

"As long as her sister is okay with it, then yes, I would be honored to have you borrow something of Melissa's." My voice breaks and I can't believe my proposal has gone in this direction. It's more epic than I could have ever planned. "I love you, Jemma."

Jemma stands up and comes around to my side of the table to sit on my lap, ignoring the table of fine China that's in the way. She wraps her arms around my neck and looks me square in the eyes. "I love you too, Walker. Every single part of you."

***Please follow Marika Ray on Amazon to be alerted when her next sweet romance, Home Run Fiancé, in the Faking It series releases.

ABOUT THE AUTHOR

Thank you so much for reading my sweet romance novel! If you loved it, please support the Faking It series by leaving a review on Amazon and Goodreads. And hey, while you're there, hit the Follow button so you know when I release more books in this series!

If you'd like to know more about me or the other novels I'm writing, please come stalk find me on Facebook, or my private Reader Group. You can also join my mailing list for bimonthly emails with personal news, bonus material, and writing updates. I write RomComs with steam, along with sweet romances to make you laugh and swoon.

Sweet Romances:
1) The Marriage Sham: A Lover's Landing Novella
2) The Widower's Girlfriend - Faking It series #1
3) Home Run Fiance - Faking It series #2 - releasing June 2019

RomComs (Steamy):
1) The Missing Ingredient - Reality of Love #1
2) Mom-Com - Reality of Love #2 - releasing May 23, 2019
3) Happy New You

Beach Squad Series (Steamy Romance):
1) Sweet Dreams - Beach Squad #1
2) Beach B!tch - Beach Squad #2

HOME RUN FIANCÉ - SNEAK PEEK

February

Jake

I've reached my breaking point.

Slamming the door to my condo shut behind me, I tug on my collar, feeling like I can't take a full breath into my lungs. The silk tie slides through my fingers as I grapple with it. I need it off my neck right freaking now. Asher's already on a phone call, either with his assistant to get a statement out to the press right away, or to my team's manager with the news. The tie finally cooperates and I toss it onto the glass table. My suit jacket follows, a crumpled heap that would make my tailor faint. I really shouldn't wrinkle a three thousand dollar suit—I'm not that big of a primadonna—but today has been an exceptionally frustrating day.

I shouldn't even be in a suit. I should be out at the batting cages with my teammates, getting ready for spring training. Right before Thanksgiving, a woman I'd gone on a couple dates with went to the press and told them she was pregnant with my baby, and as her side of the story went, when she'd told me the news, I'd dumped her and refused to have anything to do with her.

The accusation was so preposterous, I laughed when I first heard it, thinking Asher, my agent, was pulling a prank on me. Her and I were so casual I hesitated to even call us dating. We'd met through a mutual friend at a party and had gone to a few social events together when I needed a date and she wanted a nice evening out on the fancy side of town. It was entirely mutual to go our separate ways as we had zero chemistry. We hadn't even taken things farther than a simple peck on the cheek at the end of our "dates."

I'm foggy on anatomy and physiology, but I'm pretty sure you can't get pregnant from a kiss on the cheek. I'd told everything to Asher, and to the press, but I found myself having to hire a legal team and appear in court when she didn't immediately drop it. After shelling out the cash for a non-invasive DNA test, we'd shown up in court that morning to learn the results.

She'd burst into tears when the judge read the baby wasn't mine. He'd given her a stern talking to, suspecting she'd only made the accusation because she thought she could shake me down for some money.

I could barely look at her. I just thanked the judge for his time and walked out of the court house to flashing cameras, head held high.

Didn't stop me from being frustrated though.

I'm so sick of women using my professional athlete status for their own gain. Jake Kersh is no longer a guy who likes to play baseball. I'm a commodity, a celebrity of sorts, to be used and discarded at whim.

"Yeah, that sounds perfect. Release it immediately." Asher hangs up and flops down onto the opposite end of the black leather couch. He's already re-dialing. "Gotta call Joe."

I lay my head back on the couch cushion and close my eyes. One measured breath at a time brought my adrenaline down slowly but surely just like in the early days when I'd be petrified to take the field. Back then I would have never thought I'd need the same technique for a situation like this. Back then, I just wanted to play the game. Still wanted to just play the game, but when you've gone to the World Series twice and hit home runs on the regular, you got famous enough to be recognized on the street and things changed.

Asher droned on and on to Joe, the General Manager of the Los Angeles Dangers, the professional baseball team I played for. They hadn't been happy about the accusations either, telling me to get it taken care of without tarnishing their reputation and then get my head back in the game.

Thank goodness for Asher. He's been my agent for ten years and I couldn't be in this profession without him. We'd been in an elevator together in the same hotel, on our way to my high school's baseball award ceremony ten years ago. He was just starting out as a sports agent, visiting with high school athlete hopefuls, trying to score some clients even if it was a long shot. A gorgeous girl had gotten on the elevator too, but exited just one floor down, not nearly long enough for either of us to try out a line on her. As soon as the doors slid shut, Asher looked at me and said, "How come the elevator never breaks down when you want it to?"

I'd been thinking along the same lines, so we laughed together and introduced ourselves. Right from the beginning he'd given off a good vibe. Honest. Upstanding. Trustworthy. Could have been his boy-next-door good looks, or the dimple when he smiled, which was often. He looked like a freaking cherub. Maybe it was the fact he was only a couple years older than me and really seemed to understand me. Not long after that elevator ride, I'd been drafted straight onto a farm team in Oklahoma City with talks of bumping me up to the majors sooner rather than later. After telling my mom and my brother the news, my first call had been to Asher. He worked for me for peanuts the first few years, treating me like I was a bigger deal than I was. When I got bumped up and got paid better, I made sure he was paid the going rate. Every deal that had gotten me to where I am is because of him. We became friends over the years, and I trust him implicitly

"Dude. It's done." Asher places his phone down on the glass table and looks over at me with a big grin.

I pop my eyes open and look over at him warily.

"What? Aren't you happy with the outcome?" He splays his hands out like all is well in the world.

"Happy?" Lifting my head, I give him a glare. "No, I'm not happy. I should never have been accused in the first place. I should never have had to hire that lawyer, or give repeated press conferences, or waste my time managing the press' gossip about me. Yeah, it's over, but I ain't happy."

He nods, a serious expression on his face, but I know him. He's already slipping into "placate Jake mode." I hate when he does that. Makes me feel like some egomaniac celebrity client who needs to be handled with kid gloves.

I cut him off before he can get started, hopping up with the intention to change out of the constricting suit. "I'm disgusted by women in general at the moment. Maybe for a long while. I just want to get out on the field and play."

Asher hops up too, trailing me through my condo. "I get that. I totally do. But here's the thing." He grabs my arm, stopping me just outside my bedroom doorway. "Your reputation sucked long before that woman came forward. You know that, I know that, and more importantly, Bobby Maddon knows that."

I clench my jaw, not needing this crap right now. "All of which you know is not my fault."

Asher folds his arms across his chest like he intends to stay while. "You can keep saying that all you want, but the fact remains, your reputation speaks far louder than anything you can say in a negotiation. Bobby's not going to take you on if you're known to be nothing but trouble."

"I'm not trouble!" I run my hands through my hair, messing up the carefully gelled style meant to impress the judge. "Damn women just keep complicating things and then the paparazzi is right there taking pictures at the wrong time. They don't even bother to ask me to get the real story, they just make crap up and publish it."

"Listen, I believe you. You know I do. But I also know we have to clean up your image so Bobby will believe you and be open to trade talks. You know how Texas is. They want good ol' boys, not big city punks who don't care for rules."

Yeah, I know exactly how Texans are. I'd grown up there, my family and friends were still there. And if things go my way for once, I'll be moving back there this season to play for the Texas Sliders. Don't get me wrong, I love playing for the Dangers. They gave me my first chance and stuck by me for ten years. I owe my career to them.

But my mama is sick. And she trumps everyone.

I need to get back to Texas so I can help my little brother take care of her. What good is all that money in my account if I can't be there to help the woman who gave me life?

My head feels like it's going to blow with all the bottled up anger I can only seem to diffuse smashing some balls with a wooden bat or running until the sweat pours out of me. I need to get changed and get to the gym to at least somewhat salvage the day except Asher is here nagging at me. I just can't deal with him in my current frame of mind.

I pinch the bridge of my nose and take a deep breath. I don't want to lose my cool with Asher, but I think I just need to be alone right now.

"Can we please talk about this later?"

Asher sighs. "Let's hit the gym and then we can talk later. Good?"

I nod, already walking into my bedroom to get changed.

*****

"Holy crap," Asher pants, bent over, hands on knees, looking like he's going to puke.

We just did a fifty foot weighted prowler push across the turf in the training gym open 24/7 to players and staff. It's nice being the top dog. I can get Asher into the gym with me anytime I want with a grin and a wink. Considering he's almost as strong as me, we make for good workout partners. But I always smoke him on the cardio.

I slap his butt and move over to the pull up bar. "Come on, man, that all you got?"

He moseys over, still gulping air, sweat dripping down the sides of his face. "Sorry, not sure if you know, but I'm a sports agent, not an actual athlete."

When I hit thirty pull-ups, I hop down and gesture that the equipment is all his. While he struggles through a measly fifteen pull-ups, I do burpees to keep my heart rate up.

"Dude, that's not right." Asher hops down from the bar and looks at me like I'm some sort of alien.

I just laugh. He's actually in phenomenal shape, but he's right. He's paid to do all my media stuff, not have a body like a machine. This is just what I needed. My mood is a hundred times better after just an hour of sweating it out. I decide to take it easy on him.

"Ready to grab some dinner and celebrate my court win?" I slap him on the back and toss him a fresh towel from a stack on the counter, right next to the bowl of fruit someone always keeps replenished.

"Oh, now we're celebrating? We couldn't have done that an hour ago when I suggested it?" Asher mops his face and neck, the grin on his face giving him away.

"Please. You love working out here and getting your butt kicked. Just admit it already."

"I admit nothing. Chinese or pizza?"

We walk out of the gym into the fading light of a winter day in Los Angeles. I pull my hat over my head and automatically hunch over a bit, hoping to go unrecognizable as we walk to my SUV. The LA fans go crazy for their team and while I love it, I also wish to go incognito sometimes.

I snort. "That stuff's crap. We should—"

"Please don't with the Lamborghini analogy. I've heard it one too many times. You gotta eat some healthy crap to feed the machine, I know, I know. Where to?"

I smile threatens to hit my face. "How about that organic salad place you said you liked."

After I unlock my Escalade with a beep, Asher slides into the passenger seat. "I didn't say I liked it. I said it wasn't as bad as some of the other organic, vegan, raw, whatever places you've taken me before."

"I don't eat vegan," I bark.

Asher side-eyes me. "Easy, killer."

He should know better than to say anything to remind me of that woman. The woman I'd actually dated and had feelings for during my time in the minor leagues. She was a broke actress going to auditions for commercials, television extras, basically anything to get her break. I was thinking of asking her to move in with me when Asher confronted me one day, telling me he'd seen her out to lunch with some guy. Being suspicious, he'd followed her and gotten a grainy cell phone pic of them making out in his fancy Jaguar.

Being young and trusting, I hadn't believed him. I confronted her anyway, wanting a plausible explanation, and she'd admitted she'd been sleeping with a television producer, like it was no big deal. Like that was expected behavior in Hollywood. Despite living in L.A. and eating, sleeping, breathing the goal of making it into the majors instead of the Class-A team in Rancho Cucamonga, I was still just a kid from Texas. That kind of relationship was the exact opposite of what I wanted. We broke up, she hadn't taken it well, and Asher had to take out a restraining order to keep her away from me.

I'm back to clenching my jaw and trying to hold onto the feel-good endorphins from my workout. That was not a happy time in my life and it goes without saying I'd don't like to talk about it. Asher can get away with it, being one of my best friends, but even so, I'm not happy about it.

"You know not all women are out to get you, right?" Asher's voice is quiet, all teasing gone.

I shake my head and start driving to the restaurant. "I don't know about that. I've run into some real pieces of work. I'm just not sure a person in my position can really trust anyone totally, you know?"

Glancing over, Asher presses his lips together and looks as grim as I feel. "Maybe now's not the best time to bring this up, but I have an idea to help you get to Texas."

That isn't the direction I expected the conversation to go. "I'm all ears."

Asher takes a second to collect his thoughts and I'm instantly preparing myself for something I don't want to hear. Whenever he pauses like that before spitting something out, he's trying to come up with the best way to convince you to do something you don't want to do.

"The only thing holding you back from being the perfect third baseman choice for Texas is your reputation. The paparazzi have painted you to be a total bad boy, going through women like candy. Whether that's actually true or not won't matter to Texas. Your reputation will affect them. Period."

He takes a deep breath as I pull into the parking lot and slam the vehicle into park. I've already completely lost my endorphin high and he hasn't even gotten to this idea of his yet.

"This is radical, but I think it'll work. So hear me out." He shifts in his seat and faces me across the console. "Let's have you get engaged to a steady, normal woman."

He stops there and just looks at me expectantly.

I don't move, simply waiting for the rest of his idea. You know, the part that will actually make sense.

"Did you hear me?"

"Yeah, I heard you, man, but nothing about that sentence contains any logic." I can feel my blood pressure climbing and my stomach growls needing replenishment after the workout.

Asher's hands start flying in the space between as he outlines his plan in more detail, getting more excited the more he talks. "You don't understand. It'll be a fake fiancé, not for real. Having a stable girlfriend and then fiancé will help your reputation. Everybody loves a reformed bad boy settling down. Plus, with her by your side, women will stop throwing themselves at you at every function. It's brilliant really."

If I glare at him any harder, I'll give myself a headache. "What the—?" I run my hands over my beard, a nervous gesture I've tried hard to rid myself of. "Do you even hear yourself? Fake fiancé? That's insane!"

I open the car door and hop out, Asher following behind me and trying to keep up. "Come on, Jake, just think about it."

I keep stalking to the restaurant door. Maybe some food in my stomach will help my mood. "I don't know, man."

"Just think about it for now. That's all I ask."

Right as we get to a free table, I turn and look him in the eye. "Only because it's you will I even pretend to entertain this asinine idea."

Asher shrugs, complete confidence in his stature. "I've saved your butt many times before. Just sayin."

I roll my eyes and sit down, ready to get my grub on and put this day behind me where it belongs.

Releasing June 2019....

www.ingramcontent.com/pod-product-compliance
Lightning Source LLC
Chambersburg PA
CBHW061253170626
46809CB00007B/2972